THE DARK PRINCESS

THE DARK PRINCESS

ALISON BROWNSTONE™ BOOK SIX

JUDITH BERENS   MARTHA CARR   MICHAEL ANDERLE

DISRUPTIVE IMAGINATION

THE DARK PRINCESS TEAM

Thanks to the JIT Readers

Nicole Emens
Keith Verret
John Ashmore
Jeff Eaton
Daniel Weigert
Misty Roa
Carissa Sanford
Angel LaVey
Paul Westman

If we've missed anyone, please let us know!

Editor
SkyHunter Editing Team

"A genius infomancer who can hack everything under the sun should be able to remember to put new toilet paper on the roll," Hana exclaimed and gestured irritably with her hands. "That's all I'm saying."

Alison and Hana walked down a street a few blocks from her condo. They'd tried a new coffee shop that had received considerable online hype and weren't impressed. Sometimes, hype was exactly that.

I wonder if that's what people say about me.

The clear skies made for an enjoyable stroll and the August sun remained pleasant rather than overbearing. That alone made a welcome change from Alison's experience in DC last summer.

"I can see how that'd be annoying." Alison smiled. Hana and Tahir had lived together for a fair number of months now. If the only real complaint the fox had concerned her boyfriend's bathroom restock habits, that spoke well for the future of their relationship.

"You know what his response was? Do you?" The fox

flung a hand in the air as if the toilet paper roll crisis was the worst calamity to strike Seattle since the awakening of the Fremont Troll.

"No. What did he say?" Alison laughed and shook her head. "Wait. I bet it was something like, 'Be more efficient in the future.'"

Hana gasped. "Almost. He said, 'Plan better next time.'" She rolled her eyes. "Seriously? Can you believe that? Does Mason pull that crap?"

"No, he's a little more fastidious than I am in many ways. Actually, he reminds me of my dad in that way, even if he's more laid back in general. Then again, it's hard not to be more laid back than my dad." Alison slowed and frowned. A huge crowd choked the streets ahead and several police officers blocked traffic with the help of bright orange cones. A number of police drones flew overhead but their lights weren't flashing.

Hana peered at the crowd. "Trouble?"

Alison frowned as she surveyed the scene. Despite the large number of people gathered, no one looked concerned, scared, or frightened. Instead, they looked curious and excited. Many people had phones out, but that didn't prove anything other than that people were always ready to take pictures.

No. There's nothing here. I don't sense any serious magic either.

"None of the cops look upset," she commented finally. "Most of them look bored or annoyed and no one looks disgusted enough for a wreck."

A smile returned to the other woman's face. "You never know in this city."

"True enough." Alison leaned one way, then the other, and tried to find a clear view through the crowd.

A balding man stood on the edge of the gathering in a loose red shirt and turned toward the two women. He rushed toward them with a hungry smile, his tablet in hand.

He's doing everything but licking his lips. Ugh. Who is this guy? He doesn't look dangerous, but there is more than one way he could be trouble.

Alison stopped and waited for him. She doubted that he would launch a vicious assassination attempt with a tablet, and she didn't sense any magic from him. Hana beamed a ready, practiced smile.

Speaking of dangerous...

The man stopped in their space and looked from Alison to Hana. "Are you two talent?"

"Talent?" Alison echoed. "Huh?" She looked at Hana who shrugged with a playful grin.

"Are you represented already?" the man continued more slowly, and the hunger in his eyes seemed to expand with each word. His gaze bounced continually from one to the other. "Either by a modeling or talent agency? You're both gorgeous, so you have to have some representation."

Is that a line or is he serious?

Hana laughed. "We work for a security company."

She gave her friend a quick questioning look, and Alison shook her head slightly. If the man didn't recognize her immediately, there was no reason to enlighten him.

"A security company? I need you to guard me." He chuckled. "Damn. What a waste. If you don't have agents, that makes this easier. How would you like to make some easy money?"

She frowned and folded her arms. "Easy money?"

The fox kept a pleasant smile on her face, although a slight shift in her expression revealed that she didn't trust the man any more than her boss did. A former con woman was always on the lookout for someone running a scam.

Alison appreciated that. All the accrued cynicism from the last few years of her life didn't erase the fact that she reflexively wanted to see the good in people. That had mostly worked out for her, but she wasn't naïve enough to believe no one would ever betray her. Scott Carlyle had been a strong lesson in that.

So the woman I trust to have my back is the one who origi-nally tried to con me so she could trade me to the Eastern Union. How's that for irony?

The man nodded. "My name is Alex. I'm a producer." He gestured toward the crowd. "Through that mob, there are a few cameras. You see, we need hot extras for a commercial." He clucked his tongue. "You two are looking scorching today. We have a good balance with the sporty girl next door look." He gestured to Alison's jeans and T-shirt. "Not so much the dyed hair, but the clothes."

"My hair's not dyed," she explained with a smile.

"Whatever you say, honey." He pointed to Hana. "And the balance is complete with the club girl look here. You're both hot in different ways."

The other woman looked at her tight blue dress. "This isn't really my club dress. They're much sexier."

Alex nodded. "You don't have to do anything but stand around and smile at the main star as he walks down the street chewing some gum. Great product. You know Oritaste?"

Alison shook her head and Hana shrugged.

"It's a gum made with Oriceran ingredients," he explained. "It's one of the best-selling brands in the country." He sounded exasperated.

"Magical gum?" Alison replied. "That doesn't seem like a great idea."

"No, not magical, merely magically tasty. That's the big tagline. Seriously? Neither of you has heard of Oritaste?" Alex muttered under his breath. "The commercial will help." He held up the tablet. "I need you to fill out these forms quickly. We won't shoot for another half-hour. We're waiting for the star to get here."

"And who is that?"

The producer grinned. "You'll see. Someone famous. He's been in the news a lot."

Alison bit her lip to stifle her snicker. "I wouldn't have any idea what that's like."

Hana jumped in front of her friend and held her hands out. "Give us the tablet, and we'll do it."

He handed it over and his easy, practiced smile returned. "I'll be back in twenty minutes. Don't worry. You two don't need makeup or anything. We look for natural hotness here, and you ladies both have it." He spun and hurried off.

The fox framed her face with her hands. "Does all this eye shadow count as natural hotness?"

"Apparently." Alison eyed her cautiously. "Do you want to be a 'hot extra' in a gum commercial? We don't need the pitiful amount they'll pay or the exposure. It's not like I can pay for ammo with *exposure*."

"It sounds like fun. You're the one who used to be into acting. I'd thought you'd be more into this."

"In college and high school." Alison surveyed the excited faces of the crowd. "And it wasn't gum commercials, even for magically tasty gum."

A few people turned toward her and recognition dawned on their faces. They hastily retrieved their cameras and snapped pictures. Hana threw her arm around her friend and gave them a thumbs-up with the hand not holding the tablet.

The fox dropped her arm after the people were done with their pictures and turned to her boss. "Your public is fickle. They want pictures, but then it's back to gum. That producer's mad because we didn't recognize the gum, but he didn't even recognize you, the woman who saved Abraham Lincoln from dark wizards."

Alison groaned. "Stop calling me that. I wish I'd never agreed to do that interview if only because of that headline alone. I thought it'd help keep things less crazy, and Luke said it'd be a good idea. He said I needed to get out in front of the PR and crap."

"He's a politician." Hana spun the tablet on one finger with surprising dexterity before she took hold of it properly. "Sure, a hot one, but still a politician. They always think they can solve everything with talking, so of course he'd think it was a good idea for you to talk about DC."

"Wait. You think Luke is hot?" Alison blinked.

"Of course I do. I'm not blind. Don't you?" Her friend

tilted her head, her expression a mixture of disbelief and pity.

"I don't know. I guess? It's weird to think of him that way, though. He's like a brother to me, and I went to school with him for years."

The crowd shifted slightly and the chatter intensified. Something was happening behind the mass of eager and curious people.

Everyone wants to be around someone famous. I take it all for granted because Dad was already famous by the time I met him, and when I finished school, he was more famous than most movie stars.

"Forget Luke's hotness," Hana insisted. "I think he was right. I don't see what the problem is with the attention. We've been jam-packed with jobs since then, even if most of them can be handled by Jerry and the field support team. You'll need to loosen up with the magical hiring, though. It's been three months and we still haven't found someone. Sonya's great for technical support, but an extra witch or two for the field would make a big difference." She began to type her information into the tablet. "Or a hot shifter." She winked. "But don't tell Tahir I said that. I love the guy, but he can get up in his head about stuff."

"I know we need more magicals." Alison sighed. "But I also don't want to mess up the team dynamic. Everything's been going super-well if you don't count my dignity. Ava's riding me, too. She thinks we should have enough to field two or three decent teams of magicals—in her words, 'in case we need to take down multiple Mountain Striders.'"

"Talk about planning for the worst-case scenario." The fox tapped a little more information into the tablet. "She's probably the only one at the company more intense than you."

"Exactly, but that doesn't change the fact that the operation I run doesn't involve me training a bunch of people, and our main team are all friends who mostly live with each other. It'll be hard to add someone to that dynamic without messing things up." She released a quiet sigh as the frustration built once again. "What I probably need to do is have Ava set up some sort of other team entirely, and we'll only work together on big jobs."

Hana winked. "Maybe after everyone sees us in the commercial, they'll flock to join the company and you'll have a bigger pool to choose from. That way, you can find people who'll work out well without messing something up."

"Very funny. Do you seriously want to be in this commercial?"

"Yes, it'll be fun." She nodded to the tablet. "Why do you think I'm doing this?"

Alison looked at a couple of drone cameras that hovered above the crowd. "Hmm. You know what? It probably will be fun. It's not like we're on a job today. I'm overthinking this."

"Alison Brownstone overthinking something? What are the chances? Only two hundred percent?" Hana finished typing in her personal information and offered the tablet to her friend. "That's right. After this, we can quit the security business and start an epic career as the hottest actresses in the country. We can do all our own stunts. Wouldn't that be crazy?"

She chuckled. "It's no crazier than the Fremont Troll

coming to life." She typed her name on the first requested line. "Shouldn't I charge them thousands for my appearance?"

Having started her business already with a significant financial base, Alison found that other than making enough to turn a profit, she wasn't that concerned with earning huge amounts. Ensuring that the field support team had adequate access to anti-magic gear had eaten into her margins, but the business still turned a healthy profit.

Hana's eyes widened and she snapped her fingers. "You should have demanded your own trailer. I think it'll be hilarious once they realize they have Alison Brownstone in a commercial. It'll be crazy, like, 'She wasn't here. That's a girl who looks like her.'"

Alison entered her contact information. "Better that than them talking about Abraham Lincoln. You're right. Let's have some fun."

The director rubbed his chin as he surveyed the various "hot extras" who filled the street, an even split of women and men. "Okay, walk up the street from the initial position. When he pops the gum in his mouth, you all stop and stare at him like he's the most fascinating man on the planet. The women all want to be with him, and the men all want to be him. Or the opposite. Whatever works for you."

Because of the gum? Alison thought. *That must be some damned impressive gum.* It took all her self-control not to laugh.

She recognized the star who sat in a chair beneath a tent where the shade protected him from the August sun. It was Jericho Cartwright, a blond action star known mostly for the *Secret CIA Alien Files* series. Although he was handsome, she preferred Mason's muscular form to the pretty-boy looks of Cartwright.

"Are you ready, Jericho?" the director called.

The actor sighed, stood, and stretched with a bored look on his face. "Do I really need to say that final line?"

"Yes. It's the most important one." The director chuckled and shook his head. "And it's in the contract, remember?"

Jericho ran his hand through his hair. "How I suffer for my art."

And your paycheck. How much do they pay you to walk down the street and chew gum at the same time?

The screech of tires filled the air, followed by sudden sirens. A murmur rippled through the crowd and everyone turned toward the source.

A dark pick-up truck careened around a nearby corner and narrowly missed several people at the edge of the crowd. They leapt out of the way as the vehicle barreled past. A police car made a hard turn around the same corner but slowed immediately when the officers saw the people near the road. Above them, a police drone descended from a nearby building, its red and blue lights flashing.

The window of the truck lowered, and a man leaned out and pointed his wand at the official vehicle. A blue bolt blasted from his wand and exploded into the front of the police car, which swerved and barely avoided the crowd.

The side scraped the wall and sparks flew before the driver managed to stop.

The police officers working crowd control rushed toward the police car.

Alison drew a few healing potions from her pocket, relieved that she'd now decided to carry what she could, no matter where she went. She never knew what might lurk around the next corner, and it simply made sense to be prepared. These potions had been brewed specifically for normal humans—also a new habit she'd learned was necessary with a non-magical support team—and she handed them quickly to Hana. "Go check on the cops. Their buddies probably don't have some of these."

Her friend took the potions. "And what will you do?"

"Stop those assholes before they kill someone." Alison jogged a few feet forward before she funneled shadow magic toward her back. Her wings coalesced into existence, and she leapt into the air.

Jericho stood in his chair, a stunned look on his face.

CHAPTER TWO

Being able to fly and being able to fly fast were two distinctly different things. Alison always thought of herself as a fast flyer, but if she tried to pursue a car on an open highway, she might not be able to shunt enough magic into her wings to keep up.

Fortunately, the traffic in the city kept the truck's speed reasonable, and she was able to close on it, along with several police drones.

Flying around as basically a magical jet still uses a lot of fuel. That makes sense. Otherwise, the older Drow wouldn't bother with portals. It's always good to be reminded that all the money I spent on the helicopter wasn't wasted.

But that doesn't do me any good now. I could wait for AET, but these guys already tried to kill cops. I need to end this shit and end it quickly. The guys inside the car might be wizards, but I don't see anything that looks like a shield around the vehicle.

It's time for a plan.

Alison took a deep breath and poured more magic into her flight. It would be easy to simply blast the truck, but it still raced down a busy street and that kind of damage would cause a major car wreck. Inevitably, innocent people would be hurt. She retained a major advantage in that the men in the truck didn't seem to realize she had followed them. No one had even attempted to fire at her with a gun or a wand.

This could work. They've eliminated the closest cops, and they probably feel cocky. I simply need to wait for an opportunity and take it.

The truck roared around a corner and cut several other cars off in the process. She winced as brakes squealed and several vehicles collided. Even in low-speed collisions, people would need to go to the hospital, so there were bound to be injuries in this one.

"Damn it," she muttered and the wind swallowed her words. "These assholes don't care. It's time to finish this."

She lowered her altitude. Her entire body thrummed with not only the magic that flowed through her but the excitement that now boiled up. She was like an eagle ready to pounce on her prey.

Maybe I'm enjoying this takedown a little too much. That's not such a bad thing, though. Mom did it for the excitement and Dad simply wanted to do his part and make a buck, but it's not like either of them hated this kind of thing.

The truck screeched around another corner onto a new street. Alison's breath caught. There were no cars for miles.

It's now or never.

The need to now fly at top speed already took most of her concentration, but she managed to gather magic into a crackling orb over several seconds before she rocketed toward the truck. The vehicle swerved as she approached.

So you finally noticed me, huh? Too late, assholes. This is why you always watch the skies.

She adjusted for her dive angle and released the attack. The orb exploded around the back left wheel of her target. Smoke and flames poured out of the rear as the vehicle fishtailed. The smoking wheel separated from the truck a few seconds later, and the body tilted. Sparks pinwheeled as metal met asphalt before the vehicle rolled onto its side. The loud grinding echoed among the nearby tall buildings.

Damn. That was nice.

Alison looked around as she floated toward the crash. A few drones hovered nearby but nothing that looked either like a news or police drone.

Well, I'll always know how cool it was. Now, it's time to drag these assholes out.

She was almost on the ground when the back window shattered. Instinctively, she layered a shield over herself as an unseen force flung the glass several yards away to litter the street.

Two men crawled out through the now empty frame. Both clutched wands and blood streamed down their faces, but a thin translucent layer of blue light surrounded them. They looked up as she landed behind the truck and extended a shadow blade.

Alison pointed the sword at the men. "Hi. I'm the woman who blew your truck up. Actually, I'm already really pissed at you because you tried to kill some cops, barreled through a part of town filled with people, and caused car crashes, and I don't even know why the cops were chasing you. Consider this your one last chance to surrender before you find yourself on the receiving end of way more than you've already endured."

The wizards winced and pointed their wands at Alison. A few glass and plastic fragments fell from one man's hair.

"You were lucky, bitch," he snarled, but the pain in his face drained most of the menace away. "But we're ready for you now."

Why do they always have to be so damned stupid?

"This will sound really pompous," she began, "but it'll save us both some trouble, so I'll say it anyway. Don't you know who I am? I honestly thought the shadow wings and blade would be a dead giveaway. They're my trademark, after all, and there is literally only one other Drow in this city. If you'd run into her, she would have killed you already."

One of the wizards narrowed his eyes as he scrutinized her intently. His head slumped and his wand clattered to the ground. "Oh, fuck my luck. I can't believe this shit."

"What?" his companion asked, his wand still up. "Who the fuck is she? We can take her. There are two of us."

The first man gestured toward her with a limp wrist. "It's Alison Brownstone, dumbass. Do you still think we can win?"

His partner immediately dropped to his knees and put his hands behind his head.

"We surrender," his friend said as he joined him.

Alison gave them a warm smile. "See. Sometimes, this stuff doesn't have to involve too much pain. Now, you'll wait here until the police arrive so they can drag your asses off to jail for all the many, many crimes you've committed in the last few minutes alone."

Her phone chimed, and she pulled it from her pocket with her free hand, her sword still pointed at the men with the other. It was a text from Hana.

I had to give them the potions to be sure, but the cops are okay now.

Alison's smile faded slowly. "You could have killed a lot of people today. I hope whatever bullshit you were doing was worth it."

"Before I comment on what you told me, I want to say this salmon is great, A." Mason picked his wine glass up and swirled the light pink rosé inside before he took a sip. "I'm glad you haven't let yourself be seduced by the idea of spicing things up with magic. Let the ingredients speak for themselves. You're getting damned good."

They were having dinner at Mason's apartment, a nice poached salmon and sautéed garlic asparagus.

There's nothing better than having so much fresh seafood to choose from. It almost makes this too easy. I'm glad he liked it, but...wait. Something's off.

Alison took a bite of her salmon and regarded her boyfriend with suspicion. "I appreciate the compliment, but why are you buttering me up?"

"I'm merely trying to keep my favorite savior of presidents from being angry." Mason grinned playfully.

"Hana put you up to that, didn't she?" She attacked her salmon with her fork.

He laughed. "I don't get you or your parents. Your attitude, I mean. Most people think that being considered a hero is a good thing, but you all act like it's an inconvenience."

"It is. I want to help people, but attention means assholes try to do things like blow up my friends when I'm out of town or ambush me at dinner."

They'd had an unfortunate incident a few weeks prior. Thankfully, it hadn't ended with anyone hurt but it had come uncomfortably close.

"I still can't believe you were ready to stab that guy." His face twitched. He looked like he wanted to bust out laughing—exactly like he had right after the incident.

"I thought he was a dark wizard assassin. He shouldn't surprise people coming out of a restaurant."

Mason settled on letting a quiet snicker escape. "He was a reporter with a drone camera. But don't feel too bad. You didn't even punch him, which is probably better than half the celebrities he accosts."

Alison groaned. "I'm not a celebrity."

"You keep saying that, but it's not true. Just because you're not a singer or an actress doesn't mean you're not a celebrity." Mason's amused smirk was simultaneously adorable and infuriating. "It's good for business."

"So everyone keeps telling me." She stared at her fish, her expression a little glum. Cooking salmon was one thing she could manage that didn't result in unnecessary attention. "It's not like it's new. I remember having cameras shoved in my face as a teenager, and I didn't like it then either. Sometimes, I thought about disappearing somewhere—working as a librarian in a magical library or something—but..."

There's the truth floating up.

He waited a few seconds before asking, "But?"

"I do like the excitement that comes with removing the bad guys. I'm not an adrenaline junkie or anything, but I honestly don't know how happy I'd be if things were totally quiet. It was easier when I was younger and didn't think I had anything more special about me than seeing souls."

"Yes, because seeing souls without using a spell is so common, A." Mason took another sip of his wine and his amused gaze lingered on her face.

Her cheeks heated under his attention. "But that doesn't mean I wanted to confront anyone earlier. I wasn't looking for trouble and was walking down the street and minding my own business. I was supposed to be in a commercial."

"That's right. What gum was it? You didn't tell me earlier."

"Oritaste."

"Magically tasty," Mason declared before he made a disgusted face. "That gum needs real magic. I've had it a few times and I didn't like it at all. Maybe it's more suited to an elf palate or something, but I haven't seen many elves chewing gum." His brow furrowed slightly and his lips pinched. "I can't tell you what you should have done with your life, but I am interested in your future."

Alison decided to forego another bite of her salmon and focus on her boyfriend. Her heart rate kicked up at the subtle shift on his face.

"What about my future?" she asked softly.

"Our future. Our immediate future." He slid his hand across the table to take hers. "We should move in together, A. We've been seeing each other long enough."

She sighed. If the truth be told, she'd expected this ever since Hana had moved in with Tahir.

"I don't know." She shrugged. "I honestly don't. I'm still half-convinced I should set up an apartment in the Brownstone Building and move there. All this stuff with the dark wizards over the last year has me worried."

He withdrew his hand, faint disappointment in his eyes. "And they've not tried anything in months. You can't always be *on*, A. If you live at the Brownstone Building, you'll burn yourself out. You're not the only person in this country responsible for stopping rogue dark wizards, you know. Shit. There are entire government agencies dedicated to that kind of thing."

"True, but I also have to consider Sonya." Alison sucked in a deep breath as she considered the teenager's growth in the last few months. "She's come out of her shell a lot, but she needs stability, especially after everything she's been through."

"Wait." Mason blinked. Confusion suffused his face and pushed the disappointment out. "Are you using Sonya as an excuse to not move in with me?"

"It's not an excuse. It's the truth."

"She's Tahir's apprentice. Shouldn't she live with him and Hana? I get that he's not the cuddliest guy in the world, but if you want the girl to learn how to be social, being around Hana is her best bet."

"There's more space at my place." Alison gestured around the dining room, even though it was Mason's.

His stare remained locked on her for a few seconds before he spoke again. "We could always get a new place—a bigger place—rather than you moving into my place or me moving into yours. Add a room, and Sonya could stay there."

How do I explain things without pissing him off?

She drew a deep breath. "We could, but—"

"You don't want to." Mason completed the sentence before she could. "Because you're unsure about everything from dark wizards to your feelings."

"It's not that I'm unsure of my feelings," she clarified. She grabbed her wine glass and gulped a little liquid courage.

He raised an eyebrow and a playful smile finally returned to his face. "You seem nervous, A."

Alison lowered her glass a few inches from her mouth. "I love you too if that's what you want to hear."

His smile grew wider. "Now we're making progress, aren't we?"

"But that doesn't mean I'm ready to move in with you." She returned the glass to her lips to finish off the rest of the wine.

I can't tell if this is going well or not.

Mason nodded slowly. "I've realized that our relationship is a lot like my workout."

She set the now empty glass on the table. "Huh? Meaning what?"

"As long as I make some progress overall, I don't care about a few short-term plateaus." He leaned back and looked far too pleased with himself for her to be comfortable. "And today was progress. It's like I told you with the love thing, A. I'm willing to wait until you're ready."

"I'm not trying to be a bitch."

"I know." He picked up his fork. "But I'd better finish

some of this delicious fish before it gets too cold. I can't have the woman I love putting effort into a meal only for me to not do my best to appreciate it."

He might be laying it on a little thick, but he also seems happy. I got damned lucky with him.

CHAPTER THREE

Alison frowned as she set a tablet down on her office desk. The report and notes on the device didn't please her, despite the fact that the evidence suggested there was no major dark wizard activity in Seattle. She'd asked Tahir to send her any information on local dark wizard leads, but he'd not come up with anything useful. Her other contacts, including Vincent and Agent Latherby, had come up dry as well.

The PDA agent had relayed to Alison that the agency had disrupted operations in other locations, but nowhere remotely close to Washington state let alone Seattle. If the dark wizards remained active in the area, they demonstrated better subtlety and patience than they had in a while.

Is this the Brownstone Effect in action?

That should make me happy, but it merely makes me think they're planning something. On the other hand, I've disabled several operations in a row and they've lost a lot of people. It's not like they have a bag somewhere filled with homicidal wizards to throw out on operations. They also can't use too many merce-naries without it leading back to them. But I wish I could finish them once and all, if only for Izzie's sake.

Hana poked her head through the open door. "Uh oh. Overthinking Brownstone is on the case."

"How do you know I'm overthinking anything?"

"It's a combination of looking pissed and constipated."

Alison rolled her eyes. "I was going through informa-tion about dark wizards."

"Dark wizards? Did something finally come up?"

"No. That's it. Everything I have says they're not an issue."

Hana clapped, then rubbed her hands together. "Perfect. That means even the dark wizards don't want to mess with my awesome plans for tonight."

"Awesome plans?" Alison watched her friend closely as her stomach tightened at the possibilities.

"Dancing, girlfriend." Hana shimmied for a few seconds. "But not with the testosterone brigade. We haven't had a proper girls' night in a long time. We should go out, have some fun, and let the boys sit at home and brood."

"Dancing, huh? That doesn't sound half-bad." She shrugged and exhaled a sigh of relief.

The fox laughed. "What did you think I would suggest? We take on a few comers at Ortiz's fight club?"

"I never know where you're concerned." Alison grinned. "So, no, I wouldn't put it past you."

"Being unpredictable is good." Hana winked.

Sonya walked past the office, a tablet in hand and head-phones around her neck. Even after three months of Hana trying to upgrade her wardrobe, the teen still stuck to her hoodie-plus-jeans fashion style.

Alison didn't mind. It wasn't like the company had a dress code, and her personal sense of fashion wasn't chic either.

Hana spun toward the girl. "Sonya!"

The blonde teen yelped and leapt back, holding her tablet up like a shield.

"Sorry. I didn't mean to scare you." The fox grimaced.

Sonya took a few deep breaths and blinked. She was doing better about holding eye contact with people as she spoke, especially when angry. "Geeze, man. Don't...do that sort of thing. I thought there was a sniper or something."

Hana waved her hands in front of her by way of apology. "I simply wanted to grab you when I was talking with Alison about a girls' night."

"Girls' night?" Sonya made a disgusted face. "Meaning what? Something weird? Something involving oily men?"

Alison groaned and face-palmed.

"No." The fox laughed. "Not weird and not oily men. Dancing!" She demonstrated her moves again, this time adding a little disco point.

The disgust on Sonya's face only grew. "I don't dance."

Alison chuckled. "Not that I mind, but if we take Sonya, that'll limit the club choices."

Hana clucked her tongue and wagged her finger. "You forget the fine power of foxy charm. I can get her past any bouncer in this city. I could probably even do it using only my sweet face and words."

"You want to use your abilities to get a fourteen-year-old girl into a dance club? I'm not so sure that's a great idea."

"Sure? Why not? It's easier than sneaking in." The woman shrugged. "And if she's with the Hot Fox and the Dark Princess, she'll be safer than any teen in the city."

Alison snickered. "You're really trying to make that Hot Fox thing happen, aren't you?"

"I'm sure the underworld will start calling me that eventually."

Sonya snorted. "It doesn't matter."

She shook her head. "If the underworld types start calling me Hot Fox, it'll spread."

"I'm not talking about that," Sonya replied. "I don't dance. The idea of going into a room filled with sweaty people close together with thumping music makes me sick just thinking about it."

Hana's face softened. "Oh, I'm sorry, Sonya. I didn't think it through."

The girl sighed. "It's okay. Thanks for the offer. Besides, Alison's right. You don't need a kid to weigh you down."

"That's not what I meant," Alison explained. "I merely wanted to make sure we're not doing anything stupid with you."

She shook her head. "It's fine. I'm an introvert. And speaking of introverts, I was on my way to Tahir to help him with something."

"Sure, go ahead."

Sonya nodded politely and scurried off down the hallway faster than normal. Perhaps she wanted to escape any more of Hana's schemes.

Alison waited for several seconds to ensure the girl

was out of earshot before she spoke. "I feel bad for her. It's still hard for me to decide how much of it is preference and how much of it is from the way she was treated. I went through tough times around her age, but I'd already had years of my mom loving me. I had a baseline."

Hana stared down the hallway, a contemplative expression on her face. "The way she reacts is honest, at least. I learned from a young age to fake being happy. It made it easier, in some ways, to get stuff from people. You'd think the opposite would be true, but people want to help people who don't make them feel bad."

"And now?" Alison raised an eyebrow in question.

"And now, I am happy about everything but our lack of people for our dance crew. How can we storm the floor without numbers?" She frowned and cupped her chin with her fingers, the delicate fate of girls' night victory on the line.

"We don't need to storm anything."

The fox rushed into the hallway. "I'll ask around!" She pointed down the hallway. "Ava? How about you? Would you like to go dancing?"

"I don't dance," the woman replied immediately.

Genuine surprise struck Alison. The world's most competent administrative assistant seemed good at everything, so she assumed Ava could dance as well.

Maybe she's good at it but simply doesn't like it. I can see her being good at ballroom dancing.

Hana threw her hands up in the air. "This office is so anti-dancing." She stormed down the hallway shouting, "I will not let this office become *Footloose!*"

27

I have no idea what she's talking about, but at least I don't have to do anything.

Alison leaned back in her chair, a soft smile on her face. She always took herself too seriously. It was a good thing Hana would never let her stay that way.

It was perhaps the wisest decision to leave it to future historians to determine whether three women provided a sufficient number for "storming the floor." The trio of Alison, Hana, and Sienna, one of Ava's assistants, danced together in the club. Their bodies were soon choked in sweat from the oppressive heat of a room filled with hundreds of people.

Alison closed her eyes as she moved with her friends and the crowd. After she'd used the wish and lost her soul sight, she only occasionally missed the ability. For all its utility, there was something comforting about dealing with people on their own terms. Still, she did miss being able to go to a place like a club or a concert and drink in the sight of all the colorful emotions that mixed together. It had been intoxicating in its own way.

Even with normal vision, the thumping music and movement of so many people together reminded her of what that could be like, and she'd found herself increasingly eager to go dancing when the idea was brought up.

Free. That's what she was there. She was merely another young woman at the club. No one cared about her hair. No criminal assassins lurked in the shadows to kill her.

The last few months of jobs had gone off without too many problems. It wasn't as if no trouble ever showed up, but the company managed it with no difficulty at all.

Things are starting to calm down a lot more than they were before, exactly like what happened with Dad when his agency really got up to speed. But I don't even have my full magical team yet. Is it too early to worry about expansion?

There were no conspiracies, strange plans, or compartmentalized dark wizards haunting her. It was straightforward security work if occasionally complicated by a mercenary in power armor or a hitman wizard. The jobs left her fulfilled without the nagging doubts that had plagued her when she first left school.

Alison didn't dwell on it, but she now understood why she needed to leave DC. For all her successes, she was drowning there, falling into a dark pit of obsession with no one around to provide her a lifeline out. In Seattle, her friends kept her anchored and stopped her from turning into nothing more than the true Dark Princess, a ruthless, vengeful killing machine.

Her family helped, but they were in LA and she was determined to make her own way in the world. She was proud to be a Brownstone but she also didn't want to be under her father's shadow her entire life. Even though he'd scaled down his bounty hunting activities, he remained a legend.

The more I think about it, the more surprised I am that Mason was able to stand up to him. Maybe next time Dad visits, they can have a drink together without me.

She laughed spontaneously. The overwhelming EDM

blasting around her ate the sound but Hana gave her a thumbs-up.

Sienna smiled a second before a handsome man came up and put his hands on her hips. She looked questioningly at Alison and Hana and they both mouthed "Go!" They both had men in their lives but the assistant didn't.

With a grin, the beautiful dark-skinned woman disappeared into the crowd with her new acquaintance. Whether romance found her in the end, at least she was taking the chance.

Normal lives for normal people. That's what I'm trying to help defend in this city. It's good to remember that.

Alison wiped the sweat from her brow as they stepped out of the club an hour later. "That was fun. I'm glad you suggested this, Hana."

"It's hard to be such a genius and so beautiful," her friend replied with a grin. "In my generosity, I'm willing to share my genius with my friends."

Sienna laughed.

The fox nudged her with her elbow. "So, how did it go? You caught up with us when we texted you that we were ready to leave, so I'm not sure if that means you had a good time with that guy or not."

"I gave him my number," the woman explained. "We'll go out sometime."

"Nice." Hana rubbed her hands together with glee. "I was a little annoyed after all that *Footloose* stuff, but this night still turned out awesome."

Should I even ask her about Footloose? *No. Somehow, I think I'm better off not knowing.*

Alison chuckled. "It's funny. People always talk about meeting people at clubs, but it's one of those things I never thought actually happened. It's hard for me to imagine since it's so hard to talk in them."

Hana flexed a bicep. "You mean like meeting your boyfriend at the gym?"

Her cheeks heated and she looked away. "Maybe, but it's quieter at the gym."

"With all that grunting? As if." The fox winked.

Sienna laughed. "Thanks for inviting me. It feels kind of weird to be out dancing with the boss, but it's not like you're a normal boss."

"I hope that's a good thing." Alison enjoyed the caress of the cool night air on her skin. She might have to experiment more with body temperature regulation spells.

"It's a good thing. I've had plenty of bad bosses." The woman threw a hand over her face as a snort-laugh escaped her.

Alison blinked. "Is it something I said?"

"No, I…" Sienna lowered her hand and averted her eyes. "Maybe I shouldn't say anything."

"No, no. If there's something you think will positively contribute to the company, I want to hear it."

The assistant shook her head. "It's nothing like that. It's only that I think the reason I feel so comfortable around you is that I…um, don't think of you as the boss."

Alison nodded slowly, unsure where the woman was going with this. She wasn't insulted, but she needed to understand what her employees thought. "Because?"

"It's hard to think of anyone but Ava as the boss."

The other two women both laughed.

"That's true," Alison replied. "If I didn't have her, I'd be lost."

A bright pulse preceded a huge green explosion across the street. Another blast struck a moment later, enveloped a light pole, and narrowly missed a woman in a motorcycle helmet and leather jacket who hurtled forward. Her prey was a wizard dressed casually in a light jacket, T-Shirt, and jeans. He could have fit right in at many of the nearby clubs.

Of course.

The wizard fired a green orb. This time, he struck the woman and the eruption knocked her back. She landed hard and her helmet popped off to reveal shoulder-length black hair with blue streaks. Cursing in a foreign language, she yanked her jacket off, the front of which now sported several new scorch marks and holes. The shirt beneath was half-eaten by flame and harsh burns were visible on her chest and abdomen. The remains of the top of a harness, along with several throwing knives engraved with glyphs, had survived the attack.

The woman scrambled upright, swaying slightly, and braced herself on a nearby pole. Her wand slipped from the harness to the ground and rolled a few inches.

Alison kicked her heels off and summoned a shield and shadow blade. "Sienna, stay near the club and call the police. Hana, did you bring either the pendant or the ring? I want you to stay in this area in case the wizard brings new friends. I'll deal with him."

The fox nodded. "I have the ring. What's going on? Are

you sure he wasn't defending himself from motorcycle chick?"

She shook her head and walked toward the dark-haired woman across the street. "The wizard who is escaping is a bounty, probably level-four by the power of the spells he's flung around."

"How do you know that?"

Alison pointed to the woman. "Because that's Drysi Jones."

CHAPTER FOUR

Drysi dropped to her knees with a groan before she
fell forward with a thump.

Alison glanced down the street at the fleeing wizard
before she released her shield and sword. She hurried to
the bounty hunter's side and rolled the woman onto her
back.

"Alison Brownstone? Shit, am I hallucinating?" The
witch blinked at her.

She shook her head. "Seattle's my town, remember? I'm
not great with healing magic, but I can at least patch you
up." She raised her hands.

"I'm not in a position to complain." Drysi winced.
"Bloody hell. This wasn't a tidy job at all. Do what you
need to do."

Alison whispered an incantation, placed her hands on
the Welsh witch's wounds, and allowed the magic to flow
into them. The damaged skin knitted itself and the
reddened color and blisters faded.

The woman sat up and took a ragged breath. "I won't

lie, that was plenty good healing for me." She sighed. "And now, I'm half-naked."

"You're outside a dance club." Alison nodded across the street. "Most people are half-naked in there anyway."

Drysi flexed her fingers and stood, then dusted her hands on her pants. "It's damned embarrassing getting caught with my knickers down in front of you." She frowned. "Metaphorically, not literally, of course. I shouldn't have let that trash take me down like that." She took a few deep breaths.

Sirens sounded in the distance.

The bounty hunter groaned. "Police?"

"I didn't understand what was going on," she explained. "I had a friend call. I wanted to make sure that if it was a bunch of dark wizards about to attack people, there were reinforcements—especially if the wizard was powerful enough to take you down like that."

Drysi snorted. She leaned over to grab her wand and inspect it. "I was sloppy there. I got too emotional and didn't set things up right and proper. I'm only sorry it had to happen in front of you."

Alison looked down the street. "I'm sorry I let him get away. I was more concerned about you."

"I certainly won't complain that you made sure I didn't die." The witch held her wand directly in front of her tight face and uttered an incantation. She lowered it slowly along her shirt and harness and new, glowing threads appeared to replace the missing portions. They lost their glimmer after a few seconds. "This was my specialty when I was first taught."

"Fixing clothes?" Alison asked and incredulity flavored her tone.

"Tailoring, you could say. The Jones family were known for magical high fashion, even before the gates cracked open. It'd take more for a fancy gown, mind you, but I can fix a T-shirt." A wistful look settled over her face. "If my parents were still alive and knew I was a bounty hunter, they wouldn't be happy."

Hana hurried across the street. "What's going on?"

Alison gestured to her friend. "This is Hana Sugimoto."

Drysi finished the repairs to her shirt. She secured the wand in her repaired harness before she extended her hand. "Drysi Jones. It's nice to meet one of the actual Brownstone Security people."

The fox shook her hand. "Thanks for helping Alison out in DC."

The woman shook her head. "We both had an interest in eliminating the dark wizards, and she even saved my life there. If anything, I owe her." She walked down the sidewalk to retrieve her motorcycle helmet. "As for now, I could have taken that bloody bastard if my head was in the game, but that doesn't change the fact that he has friends and I could use a little backup. I might not have stopped him here, but I know where he's going. A little safehouse."

Her mouth twitched. "I wouldn't normally ask for help, but these bastards? They're traffickers. That's why I let myself get spun up. But I fucked up and now that he knows I'm onto him, we can't wait for the police. We need to move before they escape." She pointed down the street at her parked Triumph streetfighter motorcycle. "I have my wheels. You simply need to follow me."

The sirens grew closer by the second.

Alison extended her wings. "Hana, can you handle the cops?"

The fox nodded. "You do what you do best, girlfriend, and I'll tell them what went down here."

"Thanks."

Drysi jammed her helmet on and ran to her bike. She had barely roared down the street when two police cars turned the corner, their red and blue lights flashing. A police drone hovered over the street a few seconds later.

Alison flew after the Welsh witch and ignored the police as Hana waved her arms to get their attention.

So much for a relaxing girls' night.

Drysi parked her bike on a curb in a nice subdivision in Fremont.

Alison set down beside her. "Please tell me this doesn't end with us fighting the Fremont Troll."

"These bastards aren't dark wizards," the other woman murmured as she removed her helmet. "Not in the sense that they stand for anything but power. They're pieces of shit trash. The safehouse is a block up but I didn't want to drive right up to the door. I really don't want them to blow my baby up." She patted the motorcycle.

"I can understand that." Alison layered a few shields around herself.

Drysi raised her wand and cast her own shield spell, the slight shimmer barely noticeable. "I didn't mention it before, but of course I'll split the bounty with you right down the middle." She set off down the sidewalk.

A few curious people peeked through their blinds at the women who marched up the street in the middle of the night.

The witch chuckled grimly, pain on her face. "You keep saving me, Alison. Not that I don't appreciate it, but you must think I'm a bloody idiot."

"I'm powerful," she responded as she surveyed the area for any threats. "I don't say that to brag, but rather as a point of fact. I'm able to deal with situations that many people can't. I've trained Hana and she's tough, but she would have had trouble in DC, as an example. If there's any meaning to strength, it's in helping other people out when they need it."

"It's strange hearing you say that." Drysi pushed into a light jog. "Your father's a bounty hunter, even if he doesn't do it much anymore, or do you take more after your professor mom?"

If only you knew what Mom was really like.

"My dad is a bounty hunter, but he's always been about helping people, even when he didn't think he was." Alison considered extending a shadow blade but decided against it. She didn't want anyone in the neighborhood to freak out and call AET until she and Drysi were well on their way to kicking trafficker ass. "If he wasn't like that, he would never have helped me, even if he claimed he had his own reasons to do so."

Drysi's brow furrowed and she swallowed. "You don't make much sense to me, Alison. You're powerful—very powerful. And from what I've read about what went down with your birth parents, you have all the reason in the world to be angry."

"I'm only angry at assholes who hurt others."

"I'm merely saying that if I had your power and I'd been through all that, I don't know if I would have come out worrying so much about others. I can't say I'm proud of that, but it's the truth." She shrugged.

Alison's stared at her. "But you hunt dark wizards most of the time. Did they have something to do with your parents? Is this all personal for you?"

"Personal, yes." Drysi slipped a hand into her jacket and drew a throwing knife with a carved glyph. Magic radiated off the weapon. "My family used to have honor. They used to have wealth. Status." She laughed and shook her head. "I know Americans like to pretend none of that matters, that everyone's equal, but it's not true. I grew up hearing stories about my proud and noble lineage, but we'd lost everything even before my parents' death."

"Because of dark wizards?"

She scoffed. "You could say that. But that's why I don't understand you, Alison. You have all that money and fame already, but you're still so concerned about helping out other people. I don't know what to say other than you're a better bloody woman than I am."

"You make the world a better place when you bring in dark wizards and bounties like these traffickers. That's not something you should ignore, and I'm not that good. Even my going after the dark wizards is personal. They attacked my school and hurt people I cared about. The first big group I went after in Seattle—the Eastern Union—I went after them because there was an ex-Harriken leading them, and the Harriken killed my mom." She scoffed quietly. "Maybe everything I do is nothing more than vengeance wrapped up in self-righteousness. I depend on my friends to keep me grounded with all this."

"There are worse things for me than being a little more like you than I thought." Drysi slowed and nodded at an unassuming two-story white house with a well-kept lawn beside its driveway. The garage was almost as big as the house.

How many cars do they have? I only have one. That and a helicopter. And an entire building. Okay, questioning their lifestyle choices might be a tad hypocritical.

The witch fished out another enchanted knife. "How did you want to do this?"

Heavy curtains blocked all the windows, but they couldn't do anything to hide the faint magic that surrounded the building, most likely from intrusion wards. The presence of the spells already undermined the idea that it was nothing more than a random house on the street.

"Are you're sure this is the place?" Alison asked.

Drysi responded with a quick nod. "Yes. I hoped to capture the leader away from his friends. That's the only reason I didn't start here."

The half-Drow marched toward the front door. "Then let's do this direct and fast."

"Right. Good plan, Alison." A little mirth returned to the other woman's face. "Thanks for agreeing to help. I doubt they've gotten away yet, if only because I destroyed the bastard's phone during my first attack."

Alison reached the porch and layered additional light

and shadow magic into her shields. The level of magic on the other side rose steadily. "Do you feel that?"

Her companion moved away from the porch toward the front window. "Here, then?"

"Let me take point." Alison moved into position. "On three." She coiled shadow energy around her legs. "One... two...three."

The release of the energy rocketed her toward the window. Her shield took the punishment of the bruising impact but the glass shattered and launched shards forward with the rising curtains. The force embedded the fragments into the chest of a man with a shotgun a few feet into the living room. He screamed and fell back.

Alison barely had time to take in the five other men in the room before they attacked. Three of them opened fire, but their bullets bounced easily off her shield.

You should have brought some anti-magics, assholes.

The other two men pelted her with fireballs from their wands. Two violent blasts forced her back, but her defenses remained strong.

A throwing knife arced through the open window before the curtains fell back into place. Multiple lines of blue energy crackled from the blade and struck the two wizards once it was within range. Their previously invisible shields flashed, but they remained standing as the enchanted knife fell at their feet.

Alison ignored the gunmen as she hurled a few stun bolts of her own. Drysi's attack had already weakened their shields, and a few more attacks penetrated and finally brought them to the ground, where they lay and twitched from the magic.

She turned to finish off the other men, but Drysi leapt through the window, a knife in hand. The blade literally crackled as pure white energy danced from it. Even as the thugs continued to fire and their bullets bounced off her shield, she closed in on them. The Welsh witch dispatched the first adversary with a swift blow and immediately felled the second in almost the same motion. The men jerked several times and their eyes rolled up toward the back of their head.

"Clear the rooms, one by one," Alison shouted and rushed toward the bedrooms.

Drysi hurried after her and a makeshift stun baton swung along with her arms. They cleared the first-floor rooms in less than twenty seconds.

Alison kicked the door to the garage open. It was empty. All that space and there wasn't even a vehicle.

"Shit. Did the leader already escape?" she asked. The pulse of magic around her suggested otherwise, but he hadn't been among the men they'd disabled.

"I'll clear the second story," the other woman shouted. "You check the basement."

The half-Drow sprinted toward the basement door and blinked in slight surprise. No matter how many times she entered a basement, she half-expected them to be like that at her parents' house. A basement door without a DNA scanner and numeric keypad seemed naked.

She threw the door open as Drysi's footsteps sounded from above. Nothing happened—no traps, no explosions, no magical glyphs of stunning.

These guys obviously depended too much on never getting caught.

Alison leapt down the stairs and flared a small amount of magic at the end to break her fall. The wizard from outside the club stood in the small area, his animated scowl only enhanced by the bright light from the ceiling fan fitting.

Four gagged women knelt in front of him, all with tear-stained faces and their hands bound.

The man pointed his wand at the women and the tip pulsed green. "I'm using all my concentration right now to keep this energy in. If something bad happens to me, it'll all come out on these four pretty girls right there. And honestly, that'd be a fucking waste considering how much time and effort I spent to keep them in good condition before shipment."

"It'll be all right," Alison assured the victims softly, her attention on the scared women rather than the wizard. She raised her hands slowly. "I'll make you a deal. You can walk. I only want them."

"Do you think I don't fucking know who you are?" he shouted.

"If you know who I am, then you know bounties aren't even my thing anymore." She stepped slowly to the side and hoped he hadn't realized that she wasn't alone.

"You think I'll walk into that bitch's knives, don't you? How fucking stupid do you think I am?"

Well, shit. There went that plan.

"If you harm those women, you won't get out of here," she declared. "But if you run right now, at least you have a chance to escape."

The wizard yanked one of the women up by her hair and tightened his arm around her neck as he shoved her forward. He held his wand pointed at her head. "I need a little insurance."

Alison stepped into a corner, her hands in front of her. "Fine. Let's take it nice and easy."

"I heard you were pretty ruthless, Brownstone," the man sneered. "But all that power doesn't mean shit if you can't use it. Now, you have to make a choice. Me or the girls." He shoved his hostage toward her and flung his arm back to aim at the three other women.

Alison leapt in front of them. The wizard released his attack and a blinding green orb exploded against her and enveloped her in flame and heat. The strain of the attack distracted her for a few seconds as it stripped layers of her shields. By the time she'd regained her bearings, the wizard was halfway up the stairs.

She didn't attack him but instead, turned to check on the women. They all whimpered quietly, but they didn't seem seriously hurt other than a few slight burns.

"Stay here," she shouted as she ran toward the stairs and blinked a few times to try to help with the pain in her eyes.

The trafficker stood at the top of the stairs. His arms hung loosely from his side and his wand lay on the top stair. He toppled backward and thumped down the rest of the way before he landed, already dead, at Alison's feet. One of Drysi's knives protruded from his right eye.

The witch glared from the top of the stairs. "I'm not being funny when I say some things are worth more than money." She pointed at the dead wizard. "He tried to kill them all, didn't he?"

Alison nodded and sighed. "It's okay. They're hurt, but I took the brunt of it."

Drysi looked relieved. "Criminal scum. At least the dark wizards are fighting for something." She spat on the ground. "Of course, I'm not saying they aren't right bloody bastards."

"Let's get the police here to clean up and take care of these women."

The hostages all sobbed quietly, overwhelmed by the experience.

She drew a deep breath. *We saved them.*

A half-dozen cop cars were parked around the house and in the driveway. Police and news drones circled overhead. The suspects had already been rounded up and the dead ringleader loaded into the coroner's van. The four women victims had been taken to the hospital for treatment and evaluation.

Half the neighborhood crowded the street with their phones out to take video of the scene. No one expected this kind of thing in their quiet little slice of the neighborhood. The relatively close Fremont Troll was at least a known threat.

Drysi stood on the sidewalk and completed her statement to a detective. Alison had already given hers, and her mere presence was enough for the police not to request additional AET backup.

The half-Drow waited until the detective nodded and walked away to go over to the other witch. "Is everything okay?"

"It's not a tidy job, but the important part is done," the

witch responded with a frown. "The police made it clear that I'll get shit nothing for the dead man's bounty, but there were some bounties on the others and a reward for finding the missing women. I'll split it with you, fifty-fifty, like I said."

"It's really okay. I don't need the money."

Drysi chuckled darkly. "If only we could all be so rich, Alison. No. I pay my debts." She stared at the broken window. "Magic came back into the open, and it's made things better, but it's also made some things worse."

"It didn't change anything. It merely gave more people different tools. Magical healing is as important as magical weapons, even if it's not everywhere. Technomagic improves people's lives."

"But I wonder sometimes…" Drysi looked at her hands. "Maybe it was better when no one knew. When it was under control."

"That didn't stop bad things from happening, and it's not like anyone could have stopped the gates from re-opening. Once that happened, there was no choice but to be honest about magic."

A few CSIs walked over to the porch, their tablets in hand, and forensics drones flew behind them. They began taking pictures.

"I suppose you're right, Alison. I've been a bounty hunter too long. The whole world's nothing but a bloody mess to me." She curled her hand into a fist. "It was nice working with someone, though, just like it was nice working with you in D.C."

"Likewise." Alison smiled. "I'm not officially hiring any magicals right now, but I'd be willing to make an exception for you. We don't work for garbage. I have to be okay with the client. It might be a nice change of pace from bounty hunting."

"I won't lie, I've thought about it, especially after DC. And I'll give it some more thought. Tonight, though, I'll go back to my hotel and see what buzzing trash they have that passes for liquor and I'll get proper drunk." Drysi extended her hand. "I got lucky to chase a bounty right past you, Alison. I don't know if I'd say it's been fun, but it's definitely been interesting."

Alison shook her hand. "My offer stands. You know how to get hold of me." Her phone chimed with the last hour's tenth message from Hana.

You're on the news!

She looked at the sky, curious as to which drones currently broadcast her to the world. On impulse, she grew a pair of shadow wings and their nebulous presence highlighted all the lights from the police vehicles around. Effortlessly, she soared into the sky.

I might as well give them what they want.

CHAPTER FIVE

A few days later, Alison emerged from the Forbidden Bean, a coffee shop a few blocks from the Brownstone Building. The delicious smell of freshly roasted coffee beans lingered tantalizingly in her nostrils.

I wasn't sure about this place, but I like it. Sometimes, the Internet doesn't lie. Who knew?

A number of new high-end shops and restaurants had opened in the neighborhood in the last few months, and many of the old property owners had cashed out to enjoy their sudden influx of wealth from the rising real estate prices. Other new entrants had scored good deals, especially on some of the properties previously owned by Scott Carlyle.

There is not a single piece of crap I have to terrify anywhere around here. Well, no one obvious. Some of these assholes in suits are probably stealing some grandmother's retirement, but other than tracking them down once there is a bounty on them, there's not much I can do about that kind of thing.

Alison noticed a jewelry store down the street. When

she'd first come to the neighborhood, it'd been overrun with gangs but now, people felt safe enough to have millions of dollars of gemstones openly displayed in stores. Even if the jewelry store's security system cost millions of dollars itself, it was proof of the change.

I thought the entire neighborhood would be more freaked by the attack on us, but no one even cares that the Brownstone Building was attacked. They only care that we won. It's like they believe that as long as we're here, nothing bad will happen to them, and I can't say they're wrong.

This entire neighborhood represents my reputation and my brand. If a single person gets away with a robbery around here, it makes me look weak.

She snorted. It was almost like she was a gangster controlling her own fiefdom, but even though her efforts involved more than a little whiff of might making right, she didn't charge the neighborhood for protection.

A blonde woman with a dazzling smile emerged from a red Lexus parked along the street, her gaze fixed on Alison. Nothing about her gray suit jacket, matching skirt, and dark heels suggested a tactical threat. There was no bulge to indicate a weapon, no obvious wand, and no magic clung to her. Not only that but trying to kill someone while in heels was beyond annoying, especially if you needed to escape afterward. Alison had found that out the hard way a few years back when she infiltrated a party to go after a dark wizard target.

"Excuse me, Miss Brownstone," the woman called.

Alison stopped and scrutinized her carefully but didn't recognize her. "Can I help you?"

"Yes, you can, in fact." She advanced and proffered her hand. "I'm Jenna Jordan with the Elliot Bay Eye."

"The Elliot Bay Eye? I know them. A local news site, right?"

"Exactly," Jenna responded with a voice and smile too rehearsed to come off as natural. "You know what they say. All the best news these days is local news. I wondered if you had time for an interview."

Alison sighed and rubbed the back of her neck. "An interview? About what?"

"Just things, but not the incident the other day in Fremont—or, for that matter, the Fremont Troll." She winked.

The half-Drow didn't trust reporters. She hadn't since the press descended on her family during the adoption hearing like a pack of rabid, hungry hyenas more interested in an interesting story than how it might have affected either her or her father. It wasn't that she thought there were no good reporters, but she maintained that a good, healthy skepticism toward the media was always an appropriate default.

She pointed to the Lexus. "I'll sit in the passenger seat and you can ask me questions for a few minutes. That's it. I have things to do."

Jenna grinned. "That's good enough." She headed back to the car and slipped into the driver's seat. In silence, she waited for Alison to walk around to the other side, sit in the passenger seat, and close the door.

Huh. These are nice and comfortable seats, but I still like my Fiat's better.

Alison looked at the woman. "No questions about

anything related to Fremont the other night, okay? I don't want to be in the center of that. The more hype that comes around me, the more those women have to suffer, and I don't want to be part of that either. And no questions about my adoption or my birth parents. There's enough on the public record about that."

Jenna raised her phone. "Fair enough, but I can promise you I'm extremely uninterested in the Fremont incident. Alison Brownstone apprehending criminals is basically a dog bites man story at this point. Is it okay if I record?"

"Go ahead." She took a deep breath and folded her arms.

"It's hard not to notice how this neighborhood has gentrified since you moved your business in."

Alison blinked, somewhat taken off-guard that the reporter's first question echoed so closely what she had thought only a few minutes before.

It doesn't mean anything. Calm down.

"Yeah, so?" she replied.

"I'm sure you're familiar with the so-called Brownstone Effect. The Seattle Chief of Police has gone on record admitting it's real, as has the Chief of police of the LAPD. How do you feel about that?"

"It is what it is." She shrugged. "I can't speak for my father, but I'm trying to help this city become a safer place. I've been gifted with abilities that are powerful, even by magical standards, and I'm happy to use them in a way that benefits the general community."

"How very noble of you," Jenna replied but a hint of suspicion colored her voice.

It's not like I can blame her, but she could at least try to act like I'm not a lying piece of garbage. Maybe this was a mistake.

"I'm not perfect, but I try to leave the city a better place." Alison looked out the window at several people crossing the street. "No offense, but this is the kind of detail you could have looked up about me."

Her stomach tightened as a smile spread on the reporter's face. An interview was like a battle, and no one wanted to be taken by surprise in battle.

"There's been some talk of you running for office," Jenna stated. "Perhaps for City Council, if not mayor. Given the events in DC a few months back, some people have even talked about you running for Congress. Do you care to comment on these rumors?"

Alison burst out laughing. "Me? A politician? I can one hundred percent assure you that I will never go into politics. Luke—Congressman Shephard—is a good friend of mine from my school days, and that's why I was so involved in what happened there. I have zero interest in politics, and I would be spectacularly bad at it. I won't say I'm uniquely unsuited for it, but I'm damned close."

The reporter gave her a curious look. "Why do you say that? You seem to be popular and people look up to you."

"I'm a woman of action." She shrugged. "I'm also a woman who picks challenges that are very easy to handle compared to the political minefield. Protect a person. Remove a bad guy. Those are all problems that lend themselves to simple, straight-forward solutions. Running a city —let alone helping to run the country—isn't so simple. I'm supportive of Congressman Shephard's efforts to promote unity among the magical and non-magical populations, but that's as far as my political ambitions go."

Jenna looked disappointed.

So that's your big scoop? You thought I would run for Congress? Sorry.

"Thank you for being so frank and honest about your intentions, Miss Brownstone," the woman said finally and some of the earlier confidence returned to her face. "I want to ask you about something sensitive. It's explicitly not on the list of forbidden subjects you mentioned earlier, but you might find it upsetting."

Alison narrowed her eyes and didn't at all enjoy the implicit challenge. "Go ahead and ask your questions. I reserve the right not to answer them."

"Scott Carlyle's sentencing hearing is coming up. Although it was obvious from the beginning that he would be convicted, this does bring some closure to a vicious and personal crime for you. After all, this man was responsible for trying to take your magic away."

"Mr. Carlyle was arrested and tried for his crimes. I can only say I'm pleased with his conviction, as his dangerous demagoguery—even before considering the horrible magical bioweapon—risks pushing the magical and non-magical populations apart at a time when it's more impor-tant than ever that they work together. The fact he targeted me is incidental."

The woman's fake smile vanished. Her eyes turned cold and hungry. She stopped recording and set her phone down. "May I ask you a question off the record, Miss Brownstone?"

Alison nodded slowly. "Sure, but same rules apply. I have the right to refuse to answer."

"Thus far, you're the only one who has been cured of the virus. According to official statements, it was because of unique Drow magic that only works on Drow physiology."

"Yes. That's true. An associate of mine, a full Drow, helped me. I asked her to help others, but she was very clear that it wasn't possible."

Jenna tilted her head and stared at Alison as if judging her words.

What the hell?

"Would it surprise you to learn that I've spoken with some government officials who are looking into a cure, and they've spoken with some Drow from Oriceran?" she asked.

Alison shrugged. "I haven't followed it that closely since there aren't many ways I can help. I gave them some samples a while back, but they said that they've not found anything they can use. From my understanding, because it's magical, it's more a unique curse than a virus, so they can't simply use my blood to help make a cure."

The reporter nodded. "Would it then surprise you that the Drow said they actually don't understand how the cure was accomplished? According to my sources, they examined the other patients and your blood to understand what might have happened, and they're clueless."

Her shoulders and neck tensed. She didn't like the idea of Drow sniffing around her blood. Sympathetic magic had a lot of power. After a moment, she frowned at the implications of what the reporter had told her. "Clueless? No…"

no, I had an ancient Drow help me. It's older Drow magic, but it cured me. I'm one hundred percent cured and trust me, I'd know if I wasn't."

Jenna's gazed dipped to the phone, and it was obvious she wanted to record again. "I don't want to press you too much on this. It's off-the-record as much for my benefit as yours. My sources in this definitely did me a big favor in finding this information. But I want to be clear—do you deny, then, that you used the legacy of the Shadow Forged to cure yourself?"

"What the hell are you talking about?"

Alison moved her hand toward the door handle. She'd somehow lost control of the interview and that didn't sit well with her.

"Are you denying that, as the Princess of the Shadow Forged, you have access to literal wish magic? I'm suggesting that you wished your disease away." The woman pointed at Alison's eyes. "I've done some deep background research on you. I know you were effectively blind for most of your life, Miss Brownstone. I know you used to wear special glasses and now, you don't. I think you wished for vision and I think you wished for your disease to go away because I'm here to tell you that as far as the Drow are concerned, there's no way you should have been cured with Drow magic."

Both women sat there in a tense silence, their eyes locked and Alison's hand resting on the door handle.

How the fuck does she know about all that? Would the Drow tell a human outsider about the wishes? And there's no way the Drow couldn't have cured it. Myna's old but she's not the most powerful Drow out there.

She cleared her throat. "I'm being completely honest when I say that I did not cure the disease using a wish. *If such a thing even existed, why would I let myself suffer for so long with the virus?"*

"Oh, I can think of a lot of reasons." The reporter's mouth quirked into a smile. "Maybe you didn't even know what the problem was at first. Maybe you only get a wish a year or something like that and you didn't want to waste it."

"I'm not lying," Alison snapped.

Mostly not. I was tempted to use the wish, but I always figured that I'd find some other way to cure it.

Jenna sighed. "I'm not accusing you of lying, Miss Brownstone. I'm only explaining that as far as the Drow are concerned, what happened would have taken wish-level magic. There are, I'm afraid, some unexplained questions out there."

"If I knew of a cure, I'd share it." Her hands curled into fists. "I don't care that it's only a small number of cases. I know first-hand what it means to suffer from the disease. I didn't use the wish, and there's no wish left to help them anyway." She grimaced a second later.

Great. I just confirmed the existence of the wish.

"Don't worry, Miss Brownstone. This is off-the-record, but I can see that I've upset you, and that's not my intention." The woman picked her phone up and tucked it in her jacket pocket. "Having you on record denying any interest in running for office is enough for a good story, but if you are telling the truth, the person you need to talk to is whoever allegedly cured you using Drow magic. They obviously have not told you something important."

Alison opened the door and stepped out with a sigh. "Or maybe your sources are full of shit."

"Just because I'm a little local fish doesn't mean I'm not good at what I do. Thanks for your time, Miss Brown-stone." Softness returned to Jenna's face. "I'll admit you're not what I expected from a rich woman called the Dark Princess who flies around all the time with dark wings."

"A lot of people aren't what they seem. Keep that in mind when you're listening to sources." She shut the door firmly and walked away, her heart pounding.

I won't harass Myna because some reporter thinks she knows something, especially after everything Myna has done for me. That reporter already proved she doesn't understand how the Shadow Forged wishes work. She's not a magical. She didn't understand or her sources didn't understand.

That has to be it.

CHAPTER SIX

Hana whistled as she strolled down the sidewalk. The bright sun brought out a smile as her second-favorite pair of black stilettos clicked against the concrete.

I don't care if it's hard to fight in shoes like this. It'd be totally awesome to beat down some guy with these heels, and they already have a knife name. It's like the fashion universe is begging me to get in a fight. I don't care what happened to Alison at some stupid party years ago. Why not combine a little fashion with fighting?

They'd had a brief discussion of the matter of practical footwear in fights the previous day inspired by Alison's encounter with Jenna Jordan. Something about running into the reporter had put Alison off-balance and in a bad mood, and Hana knew her friend would tell her when it was time for her to know. The best thing to do was be available and keep doing her job. None of that changed her opinion about the potential awesomeness of stilettos in a fight, however.

Today, though, wasn't about Alison or high-fashion fighting. It was about Sonya and Tahir.

"How are we doing, boys and girls? Or boy and girl." Hana held the phone to her head but kept it turned off. She only used the device so she didn't appear to be a woman talking to thin air and so attract undue attention.

"I'm ready to go and ready to win," Sonya replied through the ear receiver. For all the girl's shyness when in person, she all but drowned in confidence when she was in her element—behind a screen and far away from other people. This stood in contrast to her mentor, Tahir, who excelled in infomancy but didn't lack in confidence regardless of the situation.

He cleared his throat over the line. "I want to be very clear of the parameters for this training exercise."

"Go ahead," Hana offered cheerfully.

"Sonya," Tahir continued "you're to track Hana down using a combination of drones and cameras. I don't care if you hack other people's drones or cameras but cover your tracks so we don't make trouble for Alison. Hana will approach the Brownstone Building on foot. I won't tell you her exact distance, but she can make it to the Brownstone building without running within an hour. If she gets within three blocks, she wins. I've already set up a spell to trip automatically when she reaches the appropriate distance. That way, there will be no ambiguity about when she crosses the finish line if you want to call it that."

Sonya scoffed. "You shouldn't have told me that. I can simply trace the spell. This will be beyond easy."

Tahir snorted. "Have a little more confidence in me. You don't think I thought of that possibility?"

"No, but I hoped you hadn't."

"I've warded the spell sufficiently that by the time you could break through and track Hana, she'd already be here, but be my guest if you want to waste time on a pointless strategy that won't help you win. I wouldn't advise it, but part of learning is failure."

Hana snickered. "Be nice, babe. Honey and vinegar and all that."

"I'm simply attempting to maximize the efficiency of the exercise," he responded and a thread of tension infused his voice.

The fox knew he cared about Sonya in his own gruff way, but she wanted to do her part, along with Alison, to make sure he never pushed too far. The girl was far more fragile than she let on, and Tahir didn't always understand that. The problem with people filled with confidence was that they tended to overestimate the confidence of others.

Sonya's laugh was cocky. "Don't worry about me, Hana. I'll show Tahir up and make him eat his words."

As long as she's in her element, she's doing okay, but what happens if she loses? It's time to show her how hard this can be without being a bitch. Operation Foxy Invasion has begun.

"I'll even give you a hint," Hana offered. "I'm wearing the same dress I wore a couple of weeks ago. The one you called the Tahir killer."

"What?" Tahir squeaked. A forced cough followed.

The girls shared a laugh.

Hana smiled at a dark-haired woman who turned a corner nearby and gave her a thumbs-up. The woman nodded back.

They both wore the same outfit—a bright red bandage

dress with matching heels. It wasn't an accident. A dozen other dark-haired women in the same outfit converged on the Brownstone Building, all at different speeds and taking different routes. It was the most dangerous or delightful thing in the world, depending on one's perspective—an army of foxes.

Tahir had left the hiring of doubles to Hana after he laid out the reasoning.

Sonya needs to learn the most important principle involved in this kind of activity. There's always more noise than signal, and the key is for her to understand that on an instinctual level. When we're out there, we're always at a disadvantage because there is always more noise. She needs to train herself instinctively to find ways to filter the signal. Every little trick we play isn't cheating. It's teaching.

Hana might not have understood all the principles of being an infomancer, but she understood misdirection all too well. It was too damned fun to pass up the chance to hire a horde of Hanas to rush toward the Brownstone Building.

It might be fun to do this more often simply to make people wonder what's going on over there.

Her quick pace turned into skipping—an agility exercise in her heels—but at least it'd bolster her arguments about their combat utility. More than a few people looked her way, some curious and some openly disgusted.

What? You've never seen a sexy nine-tailed fox skip down the sidewalk in the middle of an infomancer training exercise? Let's not be so boring, people! I don't even have my tails out.

She moved off to a side street. There were fewer cameras and she moved steadily closer. As the search radius shrank, it'd be easier for Sonya to find her if she drew attention to herself.

The girl cackled. "This was too easy."

Hana's heart rate kicked up. There was no way the girl had caught her that quickly. "You won't win mind games against me, Sonya. I'm a nine-tailed fox con artist. I'm the Empress of All Mind Games."

"Nice try, Hana, but I have you four blocks out from the Brownstone Building. I win."

The fox grinned. She was still eight blocks out as she slipped into an alley. "Do you have me on camera or drone?"

"The traffic camera down the street, but it doesn't matter. I tagged you. I win. I'm the champion. Bow down."

"Confirm with a drone," Tahir commanded. "Champions don't assume. *They know.*"

Sonya blew a raspberry. "Don't be so grumpy because I won so easily. Give me a second and I'll prove it to you."

Hana took the girl's distraction as an opportunity to duck onto the street and into a McDonald's. She earned appreciative stares from a few other customers as she headed into the bathroom. Inside, she moved into a stall and closed the door.

"Wait," Sonya muttered. "Oh, come on. That's no fair. That's not her, but she's wearing the same dress and the purse is the same one that Hana had this morning."

"Similar clothing is hardly unusual in a big city," Tahir suggested. "What are you planning to do if your target is a businessman in a dark suit? Ask him to change into a clown outfit for easy identification?"

"Hey, man, that's different. You set up fakes, didn't you?"

The fox giggled. "Now you're catching on." She stepped out of her heels before she stripped out of her dress and draped it over the disability assist bar. Her smile wide, she retrieved a black minidress and matching flats from her purse. "This is all very tactical. You know, decoys and feints and all that boring crap."

Sonya scoffed. "You can't fool me for long with a few fakes."

"You should be happy I haven't gone four-legged and darted over there through alleys."

"There aren't a lot of foxes in this neighborhood. If anything, it'd be easier."

Hana zipped her dress up the side. "Aren't we the confident one? Fine. You'll feel the full power of the Hana Army soon enough,"

"It sounds like it's time for me to hack a few new drones."

Neatly tucked into the new outfit, Hana folded the other dress and shoved it into her purse. She left the red shoes in the stall. They were her second-favorite pair because she'd purchased a second pair of her favorite stilettoes for the exercise.

Farewell, noble shoes. You served me well for all of a couple of days.

Hana retrieved a small black potion and poured it over the outside of her purse. The thick liquid spread across the fabric in a matter of seconds and changed the entire accessory from red to black. Tahir never made it clear why the potion would work on the purse but not the shoes. Even as a shape-shifting fox woman, magic annoyed her sometimes.

Tahir better not have been lying when he said he could change this back. I love this purse.

"Are you ready to give up yet?" she asked. "I have a lot more than only one decoy."

"Whatever," Sonya retorted. "This makes it even easier. I'll do a high-level search to tag all the red-dressed women and check them quickly. There's no way you'll get within even six blocks of this place now."

Hana emerged from the stall, now dark and mysterious instead of fiery and feisty. "You do what you need to find me, Sonya." She stepped into the dining room. "And I'll keep coming until I knock on your door."

Several customers did a double take, their brows furrowed in confusion as the fox strutted toward the exit with a cheerful wave.

She emerged from the fast-food restaurant and headed down the sidewalk at a brisk pace but resisted the urge to jog. Fast movement would be enough to draw the girl's attention, and Hana wasn't that far from winning. She almost felt bad for how easy it was to confuse Sonya, but Tahir was right. The girl needed training. At least by living with Alison and working with Brownstone Security, she was surrounded by people who wanted to help her, unlike Hana at her age.

Okay. Let's do this thing. It's time to be as unassuming as a hot fox-like only I can be.

Sonya cursed under her breath. "I don't get it. Where are you hiding? This isn't some weird trick where it turns out you were never coming at all, is it?"

"I can assure you she's coming," Tahir confirmed. "I don't believe in exercises purely for the sake of character building. This involves practical skills you need to reinforce."

Hana laughed. She was five blocks out now. Only two more blocks to victory. "Sorry, Sonya. I won't say squat more. It would defeat the purpose of everything if I told you that. I'm closer though—much closer. Okay, so I did give you a little hint. Maybe you should look over your shoulder every few minutes, just in case."

"You can't be that close. I've tagged every woman in a bright red dress in a six-block radius, and none of them are you. You've probably gone from building to building and timed it just right. This crap won't work on me, Hana. Keep in mind, if there's a camera around or a drone, those are my eyes."

She didn't respond. The girl's statement was true if overstated. Being able to hack a drone or a camera wasn't the same thing as having them all available for immediate use. Sonya would still need a hint of where her quarry was before she invested any effort.

"Keep in mind that true enemies are not obligated to give you any aid to track them," Tahir interjected. "And generally don't. If they do give you information, there is probably a reason, and it's not because they want to help you."

Hana resisted looking up as a drone whirred overhead

and her heart rate kicked up. A few more seconds revealed that it was a delivery drone.

That doesn't mean I'm safe. She could have hacked it.

She hummed a few bars of her current favorite pop song of the summer. "I should have bought some fries when I stopped to rest."

Tahir grunted. "What are you doing?"

"Taunting her playfully?" Hana didn't shrug. "Sorry. I can't resist."

"Fries?" Sonya's breath caught. The faint tap of her typing sounded over the line. "That helps me eliminate some areas, and now I think I have a good idea where you are, especially since it's not exactly like you're an Arby's girl."

"I dig the occasional seasoned curly fries. I'd report my distance, but that would make it too easy." Hana continued down the street. If she foxed out, she could close the distance rapidly, but Alison had made it clear she didn't want anything done in public that might cause a panic. A nine-tailed fox racing down the street would, at the minimum, lead to a few concerned calls to the local police.

"No." Sonya's cockiness returned and oozed out of her voice. "You'd want a quick stop, so no Five Guys or In-N-Out. My bet would be either Wendy's or McDonald's."

Hana admired the attention to detail but kept her voice calibrated to slightly mocking incredulity. "Or maybe I'm lying about the fries."

"Nah. You're exactly like me. You want it to be close so you can really feel the win."

The fox was now four blocks out and she paused to take a few deep breaths. The girl was right. It wasn't as if she had some huge desire to win against Sonya in particular, but Hana rarely had many challenges in recent months that didn't involve beating someone down or the occasional informant manipulation.

She missed some of the fun that came with matching wits with someone when she conned them, especially if she didn't use her charm magic. On jobs, it was too risky to use her abilities, which left her less fulfilled.

Hana ducked into a minimart at the approaching buzz of a small drone.

So close. I can do this. Okay, let's wait and then go.

She lingered for a moment before she stepped out of the store and continued down the street. With half a block to go, she broke into a light jog, a smile on her face.

A drone emerged from between buildings, dropped to street level, and headed directly toward her.

"You shouldn't have stopped talking," Sonya explained as the drone hovered a few yards away. "Once you stopped talking, I knew you had to be very close. That made it way easier to look around. Changing your clothes, though? I didn't see that coming."

"Sufficient performance," Tahir confirmed. "Next time, don't cut it so close."

"Nope. She got me fair and square, babe. It doesn't matter if it was close." Hana shrugged at the drone with a smile. "Good job, Sonya."

CHAPTER SEVEN

Alison had done her best over the last couple of days to put the conversation with the reporter out of her head, along with the worrying implications. She'd let Hana and Mason know the reporter had asked about her running for office and also probed her a little on the cure, but she'd left out the details about Myna's cure being suspicious.

It wasn't that she thought Myna had harmed her. She knew she wouldn't dare and also had no concerns that the Drow had lied to her. The ancient woman's pride wouldn't allow her to deceive her princess if asked directly. It was that very truth Alison feared.

What if she did something to someone to help me? She believes in honor, but her view of honor and mine aren't the same thing. I don't want someone's life traded for mine because they aren't a Drow princess.

She pushed the thoughts out of her head as she moved into the conference room. There wasn't much point worrying about it until she knew the truth. She kept assuming the reporter's information was accurate, but assumptions weren't always correct.

There wasn't much Alison could do about Myna. The best strategy would be to wait until they next met and raise the issue. She would deal with the ramifications then. There was a more immediate issue that had nothing to do with either Drow.

Hana and Tahir already waited at the conference room table and chatted quietly.

Alison moved to a chair and sat. "Thanks for coming. I wanted to talk about Sonya. I'm a little concerned. I've thought about her a lot this last month."

Tahir frowned. "Yes, that's what your message indicated, but it remains unclear what the issue is. I think her training is proceeding well, and she's proven helpful repeatedly on missions. If there is some sort of performance issue, I can work with her to improve it."

"That training exercise the other day was crazy." Hana put her hand on his arm. "She's damned good. Even the way her mind works is impressive. I don't always get a chance to appreciate that. With a few more years of experience, she might be better than you."

He nodded. "Good. A mentor who doesn't produce a more talented pupil is a failure. Perhaps that's why I feel so defensive about her."

"I'm not worried about her job performance," Alison explained. "She's accomplished a lot more than I did at that age." She sighed as she thought the situation over. "And, yes, she has a very analytical mind. She's doing great with the online classes. I'll give her that, but I'm not worried about her mind, academics, or magical training. I agree with you that it's going well. Better than well."

The infomancer frowned in confusion. "Then why are you concerned? Why this sudden furtive meeting?"

"I don't know if we're meeting all her needs." Alison gestured to Hana. "I have friends I hang out with. Even if they're my work friends, we still do fun things together. We're all friends with Sonya, but she's a teenager and… well, we're not. It might benefit her to have friends her age. Someone she can actually do things with."

"Friends her age? That's your great concern?" Tahir's surprise mixed with the disdain in his voice.

"Yeah. Friends. Even you have friends, Tahir. They're not a bad thing."

He scoffed. "Sonya's a rare intellect with unusual magical potential. Most children her age would be beneath her. They would hold her back for little practical benefit."

"I bet you were a fun guy in school." Alison rolled her eyes. "And you were the one who wanted to be a rock star."

"Not because I cared much about more friends," Tahir insisted. "Friends are overrated. Sonya's doing well and improving her capabilities, so I don't see what hanging out with people closer to her age would accomplish. I'm willing to be persuaded, but you need to explain it better."

Hana sighed and patted his hand. "I see where Alison's coming from. Sonya's doing better and she's confident behind a computer, but she still has trouble looking people in the eyes at times. Her social skills are lacking. You might be awesome with a computer, but you can still sit here and smart off to Alison face-to-face."

"With all due respect, Hana, Sonya's an infomancer, not

a nine-tailed fox investigator. She doesn't need social skills, nor does she need to be able to smart off to Alison. Specialization isn't a terrible thing."

Alison eyed him. *It's a good thing opposites attract or you wouldn't have been able to snag Hana.*

The fox rolled her eyes. "Talk about missing the point, babe."

"I went to a magic school," Alison interjected. "One of the best, if not the best in the country, and I learned to hone my abilities. But I also did normal teen crap, and I had friends. Part of learning to control and respect power is to establish social connections with people so you have a reason to bother with control." She shook her head. "She's spent too much time cooped up and hiding from the world."

"That might be her nature." A pained look of annoyance settled over Tahir. "You've asked her before about going to a magic school, including the School of Necessary Magic, and she's been rather adamant that she doesn't want to go to such a place. I'd argue that forcing the issue would do more harm than good, especially for something as questionable as improving her social skills."

Hana sighed. "That's true, but there has to be something we can do. I know you don't care, but we need to think of her future, not only how she helps us out on missions."

"For maximum clarity, I do want to point out that for this idea to be remotely effective, she'd need an environment where the potential friends had similar interests." He folded his arms over his chest. "Plenty of non-magicals distrust or fear magicals. Adolescents are cruel enough without risking her being ostracized for her talents. I'm well aware that her future is the relevant consideration here."

The fox cleared her throat. "I have a suggestion. It might help make things clear."

Her companions looked expectantly at her.

"Why don't we ask Sonya her opinion? She's not a little kid. If she's smart enough to hunt my sexy ass down in the city, we can pick her brain about what might bother her. Otherwise, this becomes an exercise in trying to force a stubborn and super-smart teenager to do something she doesn't want to do." She shrugged. "I don't know about you, but that doesn't sound like my idea of fun."

"I'll talk to her," Alison replied. "After all, I'm the one who raised the concern. But I still want to push her out of her comfort zone." She looked at Tahir. "If that's okay with you."

"No, that's fine." He gave a slight nod. "She respects you and your opinion a lot. She might be more honest in this matter with you than she would be with me, but if she flat-out refuses, what will you do?"

"Think of a way to convince her."

Sonya munched away at her vegetable stir-fry at the dining room table, her phone in front of her and her headphones over her ears. Her music blasted loud enough to be audible.

Alison wasn't offended. She understood that the girl could only handle so much social interaction during the day, but she remained uncertain how much of that was from her trouble with her parents compared to innate tendencies.

I want to help her, not hurt her. Hana's right. Sonya should be part of the conversation.

"Hey, Sonya," she called. When the girl didn't look up, she yelled, "Sonya!"

The teen paused the song she listened to and looked up from her phone. She managed to hold eye contact. "What's up, Alison?"

Dad was a little older than me when we first met, but this had to be as awkward for him. I turned out all right, though.

She cleared her throat. It occurred to her that she could defeat a deadly gang without a single worry but talking to one teenage girl tightened her stomach. "I wanted to talk a little about your social life."

"My social life?" Sonya frowned. "What do you mean? What social life?"

"That's just it. You only hang around adults. That has to be a drag." she shrugged. "Don't you want to hang around people closer to your own age?"

"I didn't hang around with other people my age even when I lived by myself. Most are freaking idiots anyway." The girl rolled her eyes. "I'm working on coding and magic, but they're worried about stupid crap. Who needs that?"

"Sure, I get that people can be disappointing but wondered if the problem in the past has been that they weren't magicals." Alison threw up a hand to pre-empt the girl. "I know you're not interested in going to a magic school, but maybe you would feel more comfortable if we could find a way for you to be around magicals closer to your age."

"Magicals?" Sonya made a face. "That's what you think this is about? I don't think people are lame for not being a magical. There's nobody stupid who works at Brownstone Security, and you have many non-magicals there. But I think most people are dumb and annoying. Younger people are stupider, so that means most younger people will be too annoying for me to hang out with. Most adults are stupid and annoying, too."

Alison blinked. Although none of what the girl was saying was news, it was still off-putting to hear it so bluntly stated. "I see. So if you could find a bunch of people your age who weren't…"

"Stupid idiots?" Sonya supplied.

"Okay, a bunch of people who weren't stupid idiots, you'd be interested in hanging around them?"

The girl pulled her headphones down around her neck. "No offense, Alison, but why do you care so much? You always tell me what a good job I'm doing, and now you're suddenly worried?"

"You are doing a good job, but life's about more than work. When we pulled you out of the apartment, we also took responsibility for you, and that means you're more than simply an employee of Brownstone Security. You understand that, right? I know we've only known you for a few months, but we care about you."

Sonya averted her eyes and her face reddened. "Geeze, man. Why did you have to go and make everything awkward? What am I even supposed to say to all that?"

Alison smiled warmly. "I've told you about how my dad

became my dad. I know what it's like to have life hand you crap, and the only thing I want—that any of us want, including Tahir even if he can be a bit up his ass sometimes —is to see you do well."

The teenager laughed but her gaze remained focused to the side. "Tahir's a good teacher, but you're right. If Hana wasn't around, he'd be an insufferable prick and I'd probably want to punch him in the balls."

"That sounds about right. Keep in mind what I told you about when I recruited him."

She rolled her eyes. "I'm surprised you didn't hit him after all that."

They'd previously discussed Tahir's dangerous tests and games with Alison. The months working with the company and dating Hana had sanded down some of the more obnoxious aspects of his personality without sacrificing his talent.

"But let's get back to you," Alison suggested. "Let's set magic school into the one hundred percent no-way pile, but what about some sort of…I don't know, extracurricular activity? Something that doesn't have to do with online academics, Tahir's training, or Brownstone Security? Something simply for fun?"

"But I like doing computer stuff."

"I know, and I'm not saying you couldn't do computer stuff. I'm simply suggesting some other things, too."

Sonya looked confused. "Like what, exactly?"

She shrugged, honestly unsure. The lack of a kemana underneath Seattle meant the girl couldn't even wander around and easily experience the same kind of magical world she had when she was around her age.

I probably shouldn't have her leaving the city to go to some other kemana either.

"I don't know," Alison admitted finally. "But something where you can maybe spend a little more time around people who aren't way older than you. I'm sure you'd like it more than you think."

"I'm not saying no," Sonya replied but suspicion laced through her voice. "But I won't agree to anything without specific details."

"Fair enough." She gestured toward her plate. "You'd better eat that before it gets cold. I shouldn't have bothered you at dinner."

"It's okay." Sonya set the headphones back over her ears. "I don't mind the way things are right now. You get that, right?"

"Sure, but sometimes, we don't even know what we could have until we reach for more." She smiled. "I'll keep an eye out. The worst thing that happens is nothing."

CHAPTER EIGHT

Alison took slow, deliberate breaths as her feet pounded the treadmill. Tactical room training was great for simulating battle, but even a Drow princess needed basic physical fitness if she wanted to maximize her ass-kicking effectiveness. Endurance, strength, agility —all were as much weapons as her shadow blade or her gun.

If I hadn't hit the gym, I wouldn't have met Mason. It's funny how life works out.

She smiled at the thought. Since their last conversation, she'd gone over the pros and cons of moving in with him, including his suggestion that they find a new and bigger apartment. It'd help them spend more time together, but they already worked together, and it wasn't as if they didn't see each other all day. Not that she minded, of course.

I can be myself around him. I don't have to be the Dark Princess. I can simply be Alison Brownstone. Shit, he stood up to Dad for me, and that's basically like saying he'd take a nuke for me.

If she left Mason or vice-versa, not only would she be out a boyfriend but also one of her best field operatives and her only pilot.

Have I subconsciously not hired another pilot so I need Mason all that much more?

The treadmill beeped as Alison reached her distance target and the machine began to slow for her cooldown. Alison continued to regulate her breathing and her heart pounded from the intense run.

Her concerns about Mason began to drift away as she gradually slowed. Her relationship was one of the few things in her life she rarely questioned and there was little reason to start. A couple of minutes later, the treadmill came to a stop and beeped again.

Between dark wizards and running a business, I have more than enough to keep me busy.

She stepped off the apparatus and retrieved her towel to wipe away the sweat as she headed over to a bench to take a seat. She'd already done all her weight training for the day and now, every muscle in her body made their complaints clear.

I wonder…if I did a workout and then drank a healing potion or used healing magic if it'd negate the benefit of the exercise that day.

Mason stepped into the gym, a concerned look on his face.

"And I was just feeling good," Alison muttered. "What? Did the dark wizards get on the Internet and declare that they intend to teleport Seattle to the moon?"

"Sorry, A." He held his phone up. "I was skimming a news site and I found this story posted. The good news is that Carlyle has been found guilty and sentenced to life in an ultramax."

"That's right. The sentencing was today." She had put it out of her mind because it reminded her of her conversation with the reporter and certain uncomfortable future confrontations with Myna. "But life's good, and he'll go to an ultramax, so it won't be a vacation. But you said that was the good news."

"I wish that's where this ended." Mason pressed play on the video. "Here comes the bad news."

A stern-looking gray-haired anchor looked directly ahead, a graphic of Lady Justice beside him. The chyron beneath him read: **TERRORISTS VOW TO FREE 'POLITICAL PRISONER' SCOTT CARLYLE.**

"Oh, shit." Alison scrubbed a hand down her face. "I was afraid something like this would happen."

"The controversial trial of technomagic billionaire Scott Carlyle was marked by the spectacle of the man defending himself while spending time engaged in lengthy speeches to explain his anti-magic philosophy," the anchor explained. "Various extremist organizations put out statements of support for Carlyle even before the start of his trial. Now, a recent statement by a violent Humanity Defense League splinter group calling themselves the Friends of Carlyle has authorities worried."

It's funny when extremist assholes aren't extreme enough for the other extremist assholes.

The video changed to a ranting HDL member giving a speech as the anchor's voice-over continued. "The Friends have vowed revenge and have declared, 'We will free the political prisoner Scott Carlyle at whatever cost. All who have participated in this anti-human farce will be punished.' The HDL themselves have put out a statement to stress that although they continue to support a pro-human agenda, they insist that they confine themselves to non-violent political, social, and cultural means to achieve their goals. In addition, they have disavowed the actions of the Friends of Carlyle, even if they do express 'sympathy and understanding with the sentiments that motivate them.'"

She rolled her eyes. "So, it's okay to sympathize with violent psychopaths as long as they support a man who bankrolled an anti-magic bioweapon."

The anchor broke off into a description of the various charges against Carlyle and his role in the creation of a targeted anti-magic virus. A picture of a smiling Alison appeared as they talked about her being a victim in addition to helping uncover the conspiracy.

"At least it's a good picture." Alison shrugged.

"The authorities," the anchor continued, "will take the unusual step of using portal magic to avoid any potential incidents during prisoner transfer, and the US Marshals have insisted they will have no trouble getting Carlyle to his final prison. Others remain skeptical, however, such as—"

Mason stopped the video, his expression grim. "If it was only about this Friends of Carlyle trying to save his ass, I wouldn't be worried, but all these stories mention you. They're spinning these guys up. If they don't think they can get Carlyle, there's one obvious alternative. It's not like the Brownstone Building or your condo's addresses are national secrets, A."

Alison draped her towel around her neck, mostly numb to Carlyle's continued ability, even from jail, to make her day annoying. "That's not exactly a big surprise. You all helped, but I'm the Dark Princess who took him on in his fancy technomagic armor. The whole story is like catnip for reporters." She made a face. "I only hope that when they make the inevitable movie about all this garbage, they find a better actress than the one they had play me in the first movie about my adoption hearing." She rolled her eyes.

"Are you taking this seriously?" He frowned. "We might not want to take any new jobs until this is resolved."

"I know what you mean." She sighed. "They'll come at me eventually—or come after Brownstone Security. We'll need to be ready, but I don't think we have to worry too much. I'll have Tahir and Sonya keep an eye open, and we should all contact our informants to let them know we want to hear anything, however remote, about any potential threat from these assholes."

Mason's frown disappeared and was replaced by an expression of solemn respect. "No one even knows the identities of the individual Friends of Carlyle. I'm sure the FBI will do their best to help the US Marshals, but I know you, and I know you won't want to drag a bunch of people into this."

"Even if he didn't order it, this is Carlyle's last stab at me in a way." Alison snorted. "And I won't let him have his fun. I'll contact Agent Latherby and volunteer my help. He might know something, and he's always up for a good 'point Alison at the bad guys' job. For now, though, I intend to take care of my immediate business."

"And what's that?"

She sniffed and grimaced. "Taking a shower."

A couple of hours later, Alison dialed Agent Latherby from her office to discuss the situation. She finished her quick explanation of what she knew and how she wanted to help if at all possible.

"I share your concerns, Miss Brownstone," the PDA agent replied. "Let us simply say that I think in many ways, Scott Carlyle's actions were more dangerous to the stability of this country than the more direct and bold schemes of the dark wizards. I'm pleased with his conviction and am very displeased that his fans refuse to accept his defeat."

"Do you know something? If you can point me at a place, I can take down any Friends of Carlyle without trouble." She adjusted her phone slightly as she leaned back in her chair. "I'd rather take the fight to them than wait for them to attack a prison and free a bunch of assholes or attack my building. I don't want to have to repair it every few months."

"Hmm." He drew a deep breath. "One moment. Do you mind if I secure this call, Miss Brownstone? Sometimes, a little privacy is necessary."

"Go ahead." She squinted at the phone and wondered what the PDA agent needed to keep secret.

This isn't about my phone being bugged by random freaks. He wants to suggest something dangerous and maybe slightly against regulations.

A light buzz fizzled over the line before the PDA agent

spoke again. "I'll note the following. The FBI and US Marshals express great confidence but let us stipulate that confidence doesn't always actualize into reality. If we let these Friends of Carlyle attack on their own terms, it will be exactly as you say. People will be hurt—not only your people or law enforcement but random citizens." He sighed. "Unfortunately, despite Carlyle's crimes targeting magicals, this isn't strictly a PDA matter. That means I can't do much about their particular prisoner transfer plan, but they also can't stop us from dangling a little bait. If I present it the right way, I'm sure I can persuade the relevant agencies to agree to a plan."

"Bait?" Alison asked. "What bait?"

"What bait, indeed?" A hint of something approaching excitement infiltrated the PDA's voice. "You're the ultimate symbol of everything these people hate even before the role you played in Scott Carlyle's capture and in his defeating plan. If we act like you'll present some large formal statement about the situation, the Friends won't be able to resist the chance to attack, even if they think they'll take casualties."

Alison frowned. "I'm willing to do that, but won't that mean we end up with a pile of reporters hurt? The whole idea is to avoid injuries to others."

"I'm not talking about a press conference, Miss Brownstone. Not as such. We'll also need you to be present at a particular site to ensure the hook is baited appropriately. We can claim reporters aren't allowed for security reasons. We'll do a poor job of concealing the location from the terrorists, though." Agent Latherby lowered his voice. "We both know you have the resources to sprinkle material on the net, including the dark web. Although our office has that capability, it'd require a number of approvals that might make it impractical to accomplish in the timeframe of interest. Mr. Arain, however, is subject only to your oversight, and without specific direction, our office has no reason to pry too deeply into his activities."

"Do you really think the Friends would come after me?" she asked. "They'd have to know that there's a good chance they'd fail. What's the point of sending a team only to have their asses kicked? I know they'll probably arrive with explosives and anti-magics, but that's not enough against me, especially now that I'm back at full strength."

The agent clucked his tongue. "All this time fighting so many dangerous enemies, and you still don't understand the mind of a fanatic."

"Then enlighten me."

"Perhaps it's a good thing you retained a certain innocence, but the key concept to understand is that these people think sacrifice—even of their own lives—is a minor price to pay for highly symbolic victories. It's nothing but PR for them, a mere simulacrum of real war." He scoffed. "They're willing to die for the same reason that they're willing to kill innocent people with such eagerness. In the end, lives are less important to them than ideas."

Alison brushed a few stray white strands out of her eyes as she thought over everything the PDA agent had suggested. "If this is about symbolism, then to totally kick their asses would do a lot to shut them up for a while."

"Indeed, and I guarantee that if we make you a tempting enough target, this group will do whatever they can to eliminate you. If we do this before the prison transfer, we stand a good chance of weakening them to the point where they won't attempt anything else. The transfer will be on a non-disclosed day anyway. It'll be very easy to manipulate the press in this instance."

"Fine." She opened a browser and a news article about Scott Carlyle's conviction. "Let's end this. I'll have Tahir leave a few scraps around about security holes. Does that sound good?"

"Yes. I'll work things on my end. We'll have to keep Mr. Arain's background involvement between you and me, but otherwise, it's time to prod some people into trying to kill you, Miss Brownstone."

CHAPTER NINE

M*aybe I am an adrenaline junkie,* Alison thought. *I'm so damned bored right now.*

She marched past the outer windows as she strolled down a hallway in City Hall. The annoying part of the plan involved spending the entire day waiting for an attack and occasionally wandering from place to place in front of windows to demonstrate that she was actually there. Most of the wing had been evacuated, but no one would be able to tell that from outside thanks to the disguised police, FBI, and PDA agents who pretended to be city workers going about their normal business.

From what Tahir said, people were biting on his evidence in a big way on the dark web, so this has to work.

They'd even sweetened the pot by leaking a false rumor that some of the key people involved in the security preparations for Scott Carlyle's transfer would meet with FBI agents in the building shortly before Alison's alleged statement.

At the end of the hallway, Alison opened the door to a

small office and stepped inside. Hana sat behind the desk and the *tachi* lay in front of her as she messed around on her phone. She'd elected to bring along the crystalline ring, something she'd increasingly chosen since Alison's powers had returned. It was easier to activate in the heat of battle than the pendant.

Mason lounged on a small couch in the corner and looked as restless as Alison felt.

She closed the door behind her. "Tahir, Sonya, do you see anything?" she asked, relying on Tahir's enhanced commlink.

The infomancer's drones patrolled the skies along with the police and FBI drones.

"We don't see anything," he replied through her ear receiver. "There is nothing suspicious so far. Sonya's watching the outer perimeter, but everything's normal for now. Law enforcement has also reported nothing within the building itself and the nearby sewers."

Hana looked up from her phone. "What if they don't come?"

"Then we'll have spent a day doing nothing, but at least it means no one was hurt today either." She leaned against the door and folded her arms. "But Latherby seemed confident last time we talked, and I hadn't even told him about some of the things Tahir mentioned about people asking questions on the dark web concerning the defenses that might be set up in this building. My so-called statement isn't supposed to be recorded for another hour, anyway. They might want to time the attack immediately before then because they think we won't pay as much attention.

I'll wait for about thirty minutes, then take another walk in case the Friends are still looking for me."

"I have something," Sonya shouted.

Alison wondered if the girl actually bounced in her seat with excitement. She sounded like it. "What?"

"A few minutes ago, I spotted six Seattle Public Utilities trucks a few miles out."

"Why didn't you say anything?" Tahir asked.

"Because I wanted to make sure. It's like you're always telling me, 'Signal, not noise.'"

He scoffed. "You can learn."

Sonya snickered. "I've confirmed they are actually city vehicles, but they're all supposed to be in maintenance right now. Not only that, I can't find anything to explain why that many trucks should be on the way to City Hall."

Mason pushed to his feet and retrieved his wand. Hana stood and grabbed her *tachi*. She tapped the ring three times and her skin glowed red.

"I can EMP a few of them," Tahir offered.

Alison frowned. "We don't want to engage them in the city where innocent people might be hurt." She lifted her phone and tapped a message to Agent Latherby.

Multiple suspicious utility trucks on their way. I think it's showtime.

Thank you for letting me know, he responded

Quickly, she layered a few shields over herself and unzipped her jacket to pat down the pouches of her hidden tactical vest to ensure her magazines were in place. To defeat the anti-magic terrorists while she used less flashy offensive magic struck her as having symbolic value, and if this was a PR war like Agent Latherby suggested, she wanted to do her part.

The life wizard cast his own shield and body enhancement spells before he replaced his wand in the holster under his jacket.

Hana sheathed the *tachi* and tightened her sword belt with a frown. "Were you serious about what you told me earlier?"

"Yeah, don't fox out if you can avoid it," Alison replied. "You have the ring, so that should help, but we need this to focus a lot more on the local authorities. I'm supposed to be the bait more than the reason for the win, and that extends to Brownstone Security." She opened the door. "But you do what you need to if shit gets out of control."

Tahir muttered something under his breath. "Alison, I don't like the looks of some of these scans. The lead vehicle is almost certainly a truck bomb."

"Shit." She rushed into the hallway. "ETA?"

"A couple of minutes. They're coming up 4th Avenue."

Truck bomb coming from south, Alison texted Latherby. **Have everyone pull back. I'll blow it up before it reaches the building.**

His response impressed her in its blasé simplicity.

Very well, then. Please do that.

The next event was more than she expected. An alarm blared and a woman's voice spoke on the PA system.

"Attention, attention. The building is now under bomb threat and should be immediately evacuated. Information suggests the attack will originate from the south. Please leave the building using the northern exits wherever possible."

The alarm continued to shriek and the message repeated a moment later.

Alison crouched and gathered energy for a moment. A quick release launched her through a nearby window and the glass shattered and rained into the parking lot. She grew shadow wings as she cleared the frame and surveyed the streets for the approaching trucks.

Shouts and screams resounded behind her as people poured out of the building.

Damn it. We underestimated how hard they'd hit us.

She gritted her teeth, placed her hands together, and fed magic into a growing white orb. The sobering reality was that she'd have only a single opportunity. They were lucky in that a southern approach would provide the parking lot as something of a cushion for the main building. If she could detonate the bomb before it got near the building, that'd lower the chance of casualties.

"Tahir!" Alison shouted and her already racing heart speeded up more. "Do you have anyone in the parking lot?"

There were very few cars there, fortunately. Latherby might not have warned her but it seemed he had prepared for the possibility of a car bomb. That would explain his earlier calm response.

You always play it too close, Latherby. I'm on your side.

"I don't have visuals on anyone in the cars, and the thermals don't indicate anyone there," the infomancer replied.

"Good." She continued to take deep breaths and channeled more energy into the attack. The orb was now difficult to look at directly without squinting.

"They're about a minute out," he reported. "Are you sure you don't want me to EMP it?"

"It's still clustered between too many buildings, and there's no guarantee an EMP will disable the actual explosive." Alison tilted her head to peer at a fast-moving white truck that barreled down the road in the distance. "I have eyes on them. Preparing to intercept." She flew higher but held her gaze locked on the rapidly moving vehicle.

All this to stop something you can't stop. Magic's back, and it won't go away for thousands of years. Get used to it, assholes.

The truck hurtled closer and closer.

"I'm waiting," she muttered to the listening team. "I'll try to nail the truck as it enters the parking lot. It's a good thing the cops had already rerouted most of the traffic near the building. I only need a few more seconds." She held her breath until the last moment before she yelled defiance and launched the empowered white orb toward the truck. "Come on. Come on."

The magical ball of death arced into a perfect strike as the truck entered the parking lot. A white-blue explosion consumed it but was immediately swallowed by a massive orange-red blast. The entire area shook with the force of the second detonation, and a huge cloud of rock, dust, and asphalt erupted into the sky. The shockwave hurled Alison backward and she catapulted against another window. It cracked and shuddered, and her shields strained.

She shook her head to clear it, descended quickly, and broke her fall with a quick pulse to her wings. Her feet touched down lightly and she took a few deep, cleansing breaths as she drew her 9mm and aimed it toward the burning fragments strewn about the new crater in the parking lot. "So much for not using flashy magic."

"The rest of the trucks are close," Tahir reported. "These

have a significant number humanoid thermal signatures inside."

Heavy footfalls pounded behind her as FBI HRT, Seattle SWAT, and PDA agents swarmed the area, their weapons and wands at the ready. AET was not represented. Technically, while the terrorists might be dangerous, they weren't considered enhanced threats.

Alison hastily found cover behind a car. She knew the cops wanted their chance to talk everyone down. That had been the original plan, at least, but between the explosion and the armed men and women now crouched with automatic weapons behind the few vehicles and benches, she wasn't sure how things would go down. Shimmering shields extended in front of several of the teams—portable magical defenses, courtesy of the PDA.

The other utility trucks squealed to a halt. Their doors flew open, and men ducked behind them, their rifles at the ready. A couple hoisted RPGs over their shoulders. They were the only terrorists who wore anti-magic deflectors.

They must have hoped to kill me with the initial blast and clean up a few stray government wizards afterward.

Hana and Mason made their way from around the side of the building, their guns also at the ready.

A small white orb floated into the parking lot.

Alison aimed her weapon at one of the men with an RPG. Battle tactics. Kill the man with the most dangerous weapon first.

"Your gambit failed." A voice issued from the orb. "You are to drop your weapons and surrender immediately."

She had expected Agent Latherby, but she didn't recognize the man's voice and simply assumed it was an FBI field commander.

If the terrorists only have a couple of anti-magic deflectors, they probably don't have too many anti-magic rounds.

Alison stepped out from behind the car, her gun still aimed. "And to be really damned clear—I'm still alive, so you're outclassed. Surrender, assholes."

"Free Scott Carlyle!" one of the RPG holders screamed. He depressed the trigger and the round hissed away from the launcher. The other terrorists opened fire as well.

That didn't go well.

The FBI, police, and PDA opened fire. The barrage of bullets ripped through the glass and metal protecting the terrorists.

She jumped back and shoved more magic into her shields. The RPG round exploded against the car she'd used as a barrier and weakened her shields as she fell. She pushed up and hastily put two rounds into the man who'd fired. Mason and Hana took their shots as well and picked off their targets in rapid succession, along with the authorities.

Less than a minute later, the terrorists sprawled around the demolished vehicle. Sometimes, all it took was a good bullet or forty.

Alison holstered her pistol and extended a shadow blade as she crept forward. Squads of mixed FBI, police, and PDA advanced behind wizard shields, their weapons still at the ready.

Mason and Hana hurried over to her.

The fox patted the hilt of her sword. "I didn't even get to use this baby. Boring!"

Alison approached the first truck. All the attackers lay on the ground in pools of their own blood, their eyes open in their death stares.

"What a fucking waste," she murmured. "You died for nothing. You accomplished nothing, and your cause is stupid." She snorted. "This was all about the shock of that first bomb." She pointed to the still-smoking crater from the initial blast. "But if that'd hit the building, it would have taken half of it with it."

"I have a live one over here," an FBI agent shouted. He held his weapon trained on the man as a police officer cuffed the wounded terrorist.

She sighed as she released the energy that fueled her shadow blade. "All this because of Scott Carlyle."

"He's a symptom, Miss Brownstone," commented Agent Latherby from behind her. "Merely an empty vessel they've filled with their hope. One thing I've found in my career is that the kind of men who'd bomb a building and kill anyone inside tell themselves it's for their righteous cause. But the truth is, they'll adopt any righteous cause that'll allow them to do what they actually enjoy doing." The PDA agent walked over to a body, a faint look of disgust on his face. "These men would have attacked the prison, too. They probably wouldn't have made it through the defenses, but they would have killed good men and women before they were stopped. Your willingness to cooperate meant these men died today instead of people who didn't deserve it." He smiled, and a trace of humor tinged the grimness of his expression. "Thankfully, they didn't prove exactly imaginative in their assault. Either that, or they were sufficiently arrogant or stupid—possibly both—to believe that a single, massive, frontal attack would suffice."

Alison nodded. "I don't think I've ever felt so good about being bait."

Enjoy prison, Scott. Your fans can't help you now.

CHAPTER TEN

Alison was still feeling good days later when she sat at her dining room table reading the news on her phone. Scott Carlyle had been successfully transferred to his new home, a not-so-lovely ultramax in Colorado.

It's true what they say. All you need is a little closure. He'll never be able to hurt anyone again. Sure, I still need to talk to Myna, but there's nothing wrong with allowing myself to soak in success for a while.

Sonya laughed at her phone from her place on the couch. She watched an episode of the *Misadventures of Fargo Trolls* on her phone despite the huge TV sitting on the wall.

Someone knocked at the front door.

"Huh. I wonder who that could be." Alison headed toward the door and checked her camera. She blinked in surprise.

Alex the producer stood on the other side in a wretched purple suit with gold chains around his neck. Far too many shirt buttons were open for a man with no decent chest muscles.

She opened the door cautiously. "Uh, hello?"

He beamed a bright smile at her. "Alison, my favorite gum hottie!"

"I was never actually filmed in that commercial, but that aside, how did you get into my building?" she asked and managed to hold onto her smile despite her annoyance.

"I was waiting outside for you when I ran into some neighbor of yours. Ryan? Yeah, that was it. I explained to him that I was a producer and interested in helping you with your career, and he let me in right away and directed me to your apartment. I could have called, but I've found this kind of thing works better face-to-face."

"Ryan let you in?" Alison responded, her voice flat. Sometimes, fanboys could be a real pain. She sighed and gestured inside. "Fine. Join me in my dining room."

Alex sauntered in, his confidence almost visible and his cologne overpowering. He nodded toward the couch. "Your kid? I didn't know you had a kid. Did you adopt one because you're adopted? That's cool."

"Not exactly. It's a complicated situation." She made her way over to the table and sat pointedly. "I'm her temporary guardian, and she's also basically an intern at my company."

Sonya straightened and frowned. She looked down at the ground when she spoke. "Who's this guy?"

"Alex Masters," the man declared. "I'm a producer, kid. I specialize in commercials, but I'm also interested in financing some feature-film projects."

"Woah. So you're like a movie guy?" The girl kept her gaze fixed on the carpet, but her voice made it clear she was impressed.

"That's right. A real-life movie guy. I had to stick around in town for a few days because a major opportunity walked right in front of me, although I didn't realize it at first." Alex stared off into the distance as if imagining all the Oscars his potential films might make. He settled into a chair and smiled at Alison, but the smile didn't reach his eyes. "But the real person who should be in movies is you, Alison."

She eyed the producer suspiciously. "What?"

"You have so much untapped potential and together, we can unlock it."

"What untapped potential are you talking about?" She laughed. "I'm not interested in a career as a hot extra in gum commercials."

"Don't you get it?" He pointed at her. "Even without knowing who you were, I sensed it in you right then and there. Out of all the women in the crowd, you and your friend caught my eye."

There were tons of other women who were cast as extras, though. You're laying it on a little too thick, Alex.

"Look, Suzimoto is hot too, but you're hotter," he insisted.

"Sugimoto," Alison responded with annoyance.

"Whatever. If she eventually enters the business, she can choose a new stage name that's easier to remember. But you're the package already. Alison Brownstone? That's a distinctive name. It sounds both feminine and powerful at the same time. It's easy to remember, and the best part is, we don't have to do much brand-building." Alex took a deep breath and actually trembled with excitement. "Your whole life has been nothing but brand-building."

"Okay, you've lost me. What's this about, exactly? You mentioned something about movies, but I'm not an actress."

Sonya watched in silence from the couch, her earphones down around her neck.

He pointed to the ceiling. "The top, Alison."

She frowned, openly bewildered. "The top of what?"

"The top of the business," Alex responded. "And getting you there. Don't you see? You're already naturally good-looking and famous. I checked you out, you know. You say you're not an actress, but I know that you used to act."

"A few plays here and there in high school and college. It's been a long time since I've done any. That commercial would have been my first performance in a long time."

He scoffed. "It's like riding a bike. In fact, it's better than riding a bike. You already have that *it* factor and so it doesn't matter whether you've done anything lately or not. I have connections with some big-name directors who have held onto some special projects, waiting for the perfect lead—someone like you."

"You could be a movie star, Alison," Sonya commented, her face a mask of excitement. "Wow."

Alex nodded at the girl. "Listen to the kid. She has good instincts. It's no secret that we barely have real movie stars anymore. In a world with magic, who cares about a few people who can read lines, right? But you're the best of both worlds."

"What about Jericho Cartwright?" Alison asked with a raised eyebrow.

"Jericho Cartwright? Garbage. Talentless hack. He'll be yesterday's news tomorrow. But you, Alison...you could have the kind of career we haven't seen in a long time. None of this working your way up in commercials." He shook his head firmly. "Nope. You could walk into a seven-figure deal on your first film."

Alison always wondered what greed smelled like. Now, she knew. It smelled like sandalwood mixed with rosewood.

"Money's not all that important to me," she responded in a measured tone. "Even without my business, I'm not exactly short of it."

Alex shook his finger and smirked. "You're playing hardball. Of course you are. A tough woman like you, bounty hunter and security contractor. You're not like the bimbos who show up and aren't ready for the realities of the film industry."

Yeah, you're not exactly the kind of guy I'd want to trust any career to.

"I'm not playing hardball," she insisted. "I'm telling the truth."

"Fine. This isn't a negotiation yet, but because of how current and hot you are right now, I'm sure we could talk about securing an eight-figure deal."

Sonya shot off the couch. "As in ten million dollars?" she shouted.

Alex grinned at her, his shiny white teeth as predatory as any lining the mouth of a shark. "Starting."

The girl stared, wide-eyed, with her mouth agape.

He turned back to Alison. "Like I said, the kid has good instincts. I know you have money, but everyone can always use more. If you establish a rep as an actress, you'll be able to secure many more endorsement deals. Right now, you don't have any."

"Because I've turned them all down," Alison replied. "I'm not really into that kind of thing. You don't seem to get this, Alex, so let me make it clear. I run a security company because I feel it's the best way to use my natural gifts to help people. I'm selective about clients, and I don't do it to get rich, so I don't care what kind of money you throw at me."

Alex leaned back in his seat, his gaze cold and appraising for a few seconds before the smile returned. "Like they say, money isn't everything. I get it. You want more out of life."

"But ten million dollars?" Sonya squeaked. She sighed and grabbed her phone before heading toward her bedroom, her face pale.

Alison folded her arms, wondering if she should simply throw the man out. "Money is important. I won't deny that. I'm merely saying I already have enough money to pursue my dreams, so you haven't offered me anything I find interesting at all."

"Fame," he responded. "Being in the industry isn't only about money but also about fame. Being adored. Dating famous people. Handsome men."

"I already have a boyfriend. And he's extremely handsome." She frowned. This conversation had become less amusing by the minute.

"Sure, sure. That's a good angle. We can sell that, too.

Alison Brownstone still loves her boyfriend who stood by her." He scratched the side of his cheek. "We could sell you as a wholesome bombshell. Loyal and all that. It'll limit some of your roles, but you can make up for it with endorsements."

"Wait a second. You're a producer, not an agent. Shouldn't you pitch me a particular project?"

"Oh, well, I have a little agent business on the side. I'm very selective." Alex coughed a few times. "But let's get back to what I can do for you. I understand that you don't care about money, but what about fame?"

"I'm already famous." Alison shrugged.

"No, you're not."

"Uh, yes, I am. Otherwise, why are you here?"

His smile turned into a slight sneer, but he quickly quashed it. "Despite what they say, not all fame is the same thing. You're not famous. You're infamous, but I can work with that. I can work a little agent alchemy and turn that infamy to positive fame. I can help you rocket to the top until—"

"All the men want to be with me and the women want to be me?"

"Exactly!" Alex shook his finger at her. "You catch on quickly, Alison. Isn't it better to be adored than feared?"

"Not in the security business." Alison was through with this waste of time. If she ever did go into film, she wouldn't do it with the help of a slimeball like Alex Masters. "Look, you're wasting your time. I'm not interested. I only signed up for the commercial as a little fun diversion. You saw what happened and what my priorities are."

He frowned and remained silent for a long moment

before he stood. "I understand." He pulled his phone out and tapped a text in. Her phone beeped. "That's my contact information."

That's what I get for putting my phone number on that form.

"It's not you, Alex," she explained. "I'm simply not interested in the industry."

"Fine," the producer replied, bitterness in his voice. "But if you ever want to be adored instead of feared, give me a call. We could do great things together." He ran a hand through his thinning hair, his face locked in frustration as he headed toward the front door and out of the condo without another word.

She snickered. "Why do I have the feeling I'd be around more trustworthy men if I joined the Eastern Union?"

CHAPTER ELEVEN

Myna stepped out of a swirling portal at the top of one of the tactical room ramps and Alison's heart thundered uncomfortably. The ancient Drow had called her earlier to suggest they work on healing magic since the younger woman had mentioned it as a weakness.

I'm a sneaky little bitch, but I have to be sure.

While she had told the truth, it was also a test. When she still suffered from AMDS, she'd found healing magic particularly taxing.

She'd initially feared that Myna had sacrificed someone on her behalf, but the more she thought about their time together since the cure, the more she recalled all the times the older woman had appeared to be in pain. Alison had attributed it to her advanced age, but when she'd considered it more objectively, she didn't remember her mentor presenting that kind of distress when they first met, regardless of her displays of power.

Is that why I've tried to stall on this? Have I always suspected on some level that this is what happened and I didn't want to face the truth?

Myna marched down the ramp. Her flowing skirt concealed the lace-up boots beneath it as if she did her best to bring back Victorian chic. She stopped in front of Alison. "Good afternoon, my princess. I'm pleased to be able to serve you again."

"Hey, Myna. I'm glad you had time."

"I always have time for you."

Alison cleared her throat, sure that her nervousness showed on her face. "So how do you want to do this? Slice my arm or something and then heal it?"

"You'd let me harm you like that?" She sounded more offended than surprised.

"I trust you. I know you would never do anything to seriously harm me, and in practical terms, you've had more than enough opportunities already if that was your plan."

The old woman pursed her lips, her forehead wrinkles more pronounced. "I applaud your willingness to face pain, but I think it's best we practice on me rather than risk permanent injury to you. Mistakes happen, and you're the future of the Drow, even if you don't believe it."

"I have healing potions that work for me, so they should at least somewhat work for you. Just in case, of course." Alison managed a smile. "But don't do anything serious. I need you, and you still have too many experiences to squeeze out of Earth."

"I see. Such measures won't be necessary." Myna opened both her palms and a barbed, tenebrous tentacle appeared from one hand. Her mouth twitched slightly as the summoned shadow manifestation sliced deeply into the other hand. Blood pooled from the wound. "You still require the incantation for your healing magic, correct?"

Alison nodded and swallowed once as she stared at the pool of blood. "Yeah. The only time I really pulled decent healing off without using an incantation was when I was still drawing on the power from the Shadow Forged line right after the wish and I was kind of super-charged in general."

"As you improve your shadow compression, you'll find that unnecessary," Myna murmured. "The issue, initially, is one of insufficient power. Once you've done it many times using shadow compression to feed the necessary power, you'll be able to grow the non-incantation version. Incantations for some spells are always necessary, but everything you can achieve without them will lead to greater strength in the end."

Tendrils of shadow sprouted from the woman's injured hand, converged on the wound, and pushed through the blood. Her face twitched as the blood reverse-flowed into the wound and her skin knitted itself back together. The layer of shadow over it faded after a few seconds.

The Drow held her now healed hand up, her lips and face tight in a near-grimace.

That's exactly what I needed to see. Damn it.

Alison narrowed her eyes. "I've used healing magic many times and I've seen it used often, and there's only one circumstance in which I've seen someone look like they were in more pain during the healing process than before."

Myna's white brows raised in question. "What are you talking about?"

"It was with me when I had AMDS." She shook her head. "I don't want to believe it, Myna. Tell me I'm wrong."

"I can't speak to what happened to you during that period, my princess."

She scoffed. "Nice dodge. Let me be more direct. Do you have AMDS?"

The old woman stared, her expression blank. "Why would you think such a thing?"

"I appreciate everything you've done for me, but you can't answer a question with a question." Alison stepped decisively toward her. "If I have to play this card, I will. I order you, as the Princess of the Shadow Forged, to tell me the truth. How did you cure my AMDS? I already know that 'ancient Drow healing spell' explanation is bullshit. It turns out the government reached out to the Drow themselves, and they're also clueless about how you pulled it off."

Myna sneered. "Of course they are. So myopic. Note also that they were too afraid to approach you and ask. Such cowards in the end. That is Laena's true legacy."

"Answer the question," she repeated, her voice quiet but with steel behind the words.

Her companion watched her for a moment and slight indignation gave way to pride. "You're correct, my princess. There is no ancient Drow healing spell I discovered to cure your affliction. When I examined you, it became clear to me that the kind of healing magic I was familiar with would be useless, as it had been for the Light Elves who partnered with the human doctors."

"Then how?"

"It was a different ancient magic. From thousands of

years in the past when the Drow were purer in motivation in many ways." The old woman's face turned wistful and the look in her eyes became distant. "In my exile, I've come across sources of lost knowledge purged from the rest of the Drow. I consulted one of those and learned of a ritual, one that was an alternative to execution for Drow even long before my birth."

Alison blinked. "What?"

"The idea of the ritual was that killing one who was condemned was too quick, too merciful. Instead, dangerous and harmful magic, such as curses, could be transferred to them. That way, they suffered and in their suffering, perhaps learned the error of their ways. Ultimately, that didn't matter because their pain itself also served as penance for their crimes against other Drow." Myna kept her tone casual as if discussing where she'd purchased her last pair of boots. "I simply took this ritual and refined it. You're right, my princess. I transferred your cursed disease to myself. Before you ask, no, the process isn't reversible." She chuckled. "I suppose that's not completely true. It's reversible but there's a price."

"What price?"

"Death." Myna gave her a cool look. "So yes, you can transfer the disease back to yourself if you so desire, but it will cost my life."

"You—" Alison stumbled back in real shock. Suspecting the truth wasn't the same thing as having it confirmed. "You've been in pain all this time, then. You've suffered. I know how it feels. I felt it for a long time." She took a few deep breaths as her stomach lurched. "You shouldn't have done this. You didn't ask me."

Her companion scoffed. "If I'd asked you, you would have said no."

She managed to recover a little of her equilibrium. "Of course I would. Sacrificing your life and magic for mine isn't acceptable."

The ancient Drow sniffed disdainfully. "From what I read of this disease, it doesn't kill you. It simply strips you slowly of your magic. It doesn't matter, anyway, because I'm already close to death. I didn't have time to wait for a solution. They still haven't cured the others, which proves that my actions were correct. Imagine if you'd tried to finish your battle against Scott Carlyle without your full power available. You would have been slain. The future of the Drow would have died with you."

Tears welled up in Alison's eyes. "It wasn't your call to make."

Myna threw her head back and laughed. "It wasn't my call to make? It's my life. My magic. You're my princess, true, but I still have a will of my own. If you had ordered me to do something similar, I would have complied. But if you ordered me not to, I also would have done it anyway." She walked over to Alison and lifted the younger woman's chin with a single finger. "Don't despair, my princess. When I found you, I knew I had a chance to gain some small meaning after so many centuries of mere existence. It may very well even be that I was brought to you by fate to heal your disease. Why do you weep for what I've lost? The truth is that I've lost nothing. Soon, I will die, and it's my fondest wish that even in death, I can find a way to serve you."

Alison wiped her tears away and took a deep breath to

regain control of her emotions. "You keep saying you're dying, but you also don't know when that will be. It could be five years from now."

"That is doubtful. I feel it in my soul that it'll be sooner than that. Far sooner."

"All the more reason to value every single day. To value your life." She cut impatiently through the air with her hand. "You're acting like you're already dead."

"Sacrifice for others is part of life for many races. I know enough of human culture to know most of them would not frown on what I've done." Myna raised her head, her face full of pride. "If you want me to apologize, I refuse. I would lay my life down for you. It only follows that I would lay my magic down for you too."

"Then I refuse to take any more lessons from you that require you to do magic," Alison insisted. "We'll keep it theoretical."

"That's unnecessary."

"Those are my terms." She sighed. "It's never even occurred to you that I'm not worth any of this, has it?"

The old woman maintained her regal bearing. "When I felt the residual power of the legacy of the Shadow Forged, all doubt vanished. You're young—an infant really. You still lack an understanding of the greater picture. I don't hold that against you, but I also want you to at least consider that you'll have a far greater role in the two worlds than running a mere security company. Your Drow blood is strong. You'll live much longer than a human."

Alison gave a shallow nod. She'd thought about the possibility a few times, but she was still in her mid-twenties. Worrying about how the centuries might pass didn't seem important. She had decades before her extended life-span would have any practical effect on her life and relationships.

"I will do my best to make your sacrifice worthwhile," she murmured. "I can't promise that I'll succeed, but I'll do my best."

Myna smiled. "I know, my princess. I wouldn't have made the sacrifice if I didn't think it was worthwhile. Don't cry for me. Simply continue to do what you have been doing—becoming a beacon of honor and strength."

"I will, Myna. I will."

CHAPTER TWELVE

Alison skimmed through some reports from Ava on her computer. She'd expected that she would need to throw herself back into work to come to terms with the truth of what Myna had done, but as the days passed, she was less haunted.

Everything the old Drow had said was true. Alison still didn't like the idea that she had not been told, but now that the spell had been performed, it would be an insult to her benefactor for Alison to do anything but her best in her attempt to make the woman proud of her.

Sienna knocked lightly on the door, a confused look on her face and a small envelope in her hand. "Alison?"

She looked up from her screen. "What's up?"

"This…uh, seemed to suddenly appear. I'm sure someone delivered it, but I didn't see who. It's addressed to you and there's no return address." The woman walked over to the desk and handed Alison the envelope.

Shit. A letter bomb from the Friends?

She took the envelope. It didn't feel heavy enough to be a letter bomb and small amounts of magic radiated off it. Her lingering concern disappeared.

Immediately, she knew exactly what this was. The sender, Izzie, might change up the method of delivery now and again, but the feel of the magic was always the same.

"Thanks, Sienna. Please close my door on the way out."

The woman nodded. "Sure thing." She headed out of the room and closed the door quietly.

Alison tore the envelope open and pulled out the hand-written enchanted letter.

Alison,

I'm in town and I wanted to talk to you about a few things. I don't think I'll be lucky enough to run into you on a job, so how about you show up at Maneki two hours from now?

Izzie

She glanced at the clock on her computer before she folded the letter and placed it on her desk. Flames burst from the pages and consumed the paper.

If Izzie's in town, does that mean the dark wizards are on the move?

Shigeru directed Alison to a private room on arrival. She slid the door open, and Izzie sat inside in front of a massive sushi boat, downing some tuna maki.

Her friend looked up with a smile and waved.

Alison slid the door closed behind her. Light magic radiated from the walls and door.

"Did you throw up some privacy spells and a few wards already?" she asked.

Izzie nodded and swallowed. "I know we could talk at your place and be safe. After all, your team eliminated a bunch of attackers without you even being there. But I believe that the more I keep things secret, the fewer chances I give the bastards hunting me an opportunity to catch up."

Alison knelt in front of the low-lying table and grabbed a pair of chopsticks. "This isn't a social call?"

Her companion gave her an apologetic smile. "I wish it could be, Alison, but no, this is about the dark wizards. Isn't everything about them in the end when it comes to me?" Her laugh held a bitter edge.

Alison selected some uni and savored the salty taste and creamy texture. There was something almost profane about having non-victory sushi at Maneki when it came to dark wizards.

"Everything's been quiet here," she related. "At least as far as dark wizards go. I ran into a bounty hunter recently who hunts dark wizards, but she wasn't working a job related to them."

"Who is the bounty hunter?" Izzie asked.

"Drysi Jones. She's from Cardiff."

The other woman furrowed her brow. "I've heard of her but don't know much about her."

"I'm trying to get her to join the company. She's good in a fight." She shrugged. "But I assume that if you're here, it means you've found something."

"You could say that." Izzie poured herself some sake. "I unearthed some good leads after my last trip to Seattle, and

I've discovered something new and important. I finally feel like I've made some forward progress." She lifted the sake and took a sip.

Alison nodded slowly. "What have you learned?"

"There's an alliance of several old dark wizard families behind what's going on lately. They call themselves the Seventh Order."

"Is there some special meaning in the name?"

"Some crap about different eras of dark family control." Izzie scoffed. "You know how these guys like to see themselves. The thing is, most dark families might be a bunch of pompous dicks, but they also aren't as fucked up as the people willing to release a Mountain Strider into a major city."

"What are you saying?" Alison narrowed her eyes.

"I'm saying we don't have to burn every dark family back to their roots for this to be over, merely the Seventh Order. As best as I can tell, they represent only four families. Although the other families support the goal of the dark families that control magic on Earth, they don't support the kind of aggressive shit these people have pulled, nor their alliance with Galbrathians, even though they're mostly gone now."

"That all makes sense." The half-Drow eased some snapper into her mouth. Paranoia wasn't as good a seasoning as victory.

"It gets better—or worse, depending on how you look at it." Her friend shrugged. "I don't know all the details. They're too good at keeping things separate—either the old-fashioned way or with compartmentalization—but I have confirmed that the endgame somehow involves Seattle."

Alison set her chopsticks down. "Is it because of me?"

Izzie shook her head. "No. As far as I can tell, they're more interested in getting their hands on my mother and me than you. Not to be dismissive, given how many times they've screwed with you, but I think your involvement is essentially incidental. You're an obstacle, not the target."

"I don't know if that makes me feel better or worse." She snickered with dark amusement.

"Sorry, Alison. The truth is that they only care about you in Seattle because you've disrupted their plans. They might come after you again but given the pounding you gave them the last several times, from what I can tell, they're trying to lie low and fly in under the Brownstone radar. I've heard they're also worried that if they push too hard, they might wake up Daddy Brownstone, and they don't think they can win against both the Brownstones and Berens at full strength."

Alison let an evil grin appear. "That's true." Her grin faded as she considered what Izzie had told her. "But it's easier when they get arrogant. If they're afraid, they'll be careful. Like I said, things have been quiet. Still, it's not like I'd be able to find a couple of dark wizards if they rolled into town and didn't do something obvious, even with all the resources of my company."

"Exactly," Izzie replied. "I've been able to confirm on my end that the Troll was a distraction. There was something else they tried to do that had nothing to do with anything that happened in DC, but none of the foot soldiers I've snagged seem to know what the actual goal was." She gritted her teeth. "If we only knew who one of the leaders was, we could take the fight to them and finally end this. I doubt they've compartmentalized it all away."

"You think?"

"Yes. Everything I've found suggests that if we can stop this alliance—this so-called Seventh Order—then it's over. They'll stop hounding my family, and Seattle will be safe. Whatever their plan is, it goes back decades to immediately after the gates first started opening."

Alison pointed at her friend. "Do you know why the Seventh Order is so interested in you and your mom in particular?"

"I'm not sure why." Izzie gulped more sake and set her cup down. "I have a theory, though."

"What?"

"The ability to draw on the power of our line. It has all sorts of ritual implications." She frowned. "But it's only a theory. I can't be sure and it doesn't matter, really. If we end the Seventh Order, we end the threat. We don't need to know their plan. We merely need to find them and destroy them."

"You make it sound so easy." Alison poured herself some tea. She wasn't in the mood for alcohol. "If it was, you wouldn't still have to contact me with self-destructing letters and live in hiding most of the time."

"You're right, and I also know that I can't end this by myself. Not even my family can end this. I need help. We need help."

She finished pouring and held her friend's gaze. "You know I'll do whatever I can, Izzie."

"Yes, I do. That's why I'll try to stay in contact more regularly. I'll use the same types of letters, but monthly. Maybe visits, too."

"I wouldn't complain about seeing you more often." Alison's smile held genuine warmth. "I miss you."

"I miss you, too. I miss..." Izzie shook her head, her cheeks red from her sake. "I miss a lot of things. I've almost forgotten what it's like to not be on the run, and sometimes, I wonder if I'd be happier if my true memories were still gone."

"What good would that do? They would still come for you."

Her friend sighed and leaned back, her lips tight. "I know," she whispered. She snorted and slapped her cheeks. "This is why alcohol is dangerous. Fuck all that. I simply need to destroy the Seventh Order. I feel that for the first time in years, I have serious forward momentum. I want to take the fight to their home like they took it to ours when they attacked the school and hurt people. People like Tanner."

Alison looked down and nodded. "I know how you feel. I've not been on the run like you, but I've been obsessed with them. Neither of us can move on fully with our lives until they're defeated. I agree with you. We need to gather allies. The PDA can be useful sometimes, but they're an American government agency. If the Seventh Order's base ends up in Iceland or something, who knows if they'd even help us. And they might not feel they represent a clear threat, even if you say they've targeted Seattle. And there have to be other dark wizard spies in the government."

Izzie grimaced. "Yes, I know. I think we should keep it

tight and personal. My family's onboard. What about yours?"

"I can probably bring them in. Although Dad's supposed to ask pretty please before he really cuts loose, if we go to him and say, 'Let's end this,' he will."

"Even if it puts a bullseye on his back with the government?"

"Yeah." She shrugged. "Myna, Hana, and Mason will help out. I can get Tahir involved, probably, but it's not fair to risk Sonya."

"Sonya?"

"Long story. I have a teenage infomancer living with me now." She smiled sheepishly.

"You have been busy."

"I could probably recruit Lily, too," Alison explained. "We're talking a solid team if we know what we're doing and where we're going. I might be able to involve some of the magicals from my dad's agency, too, but I'm not sure. Trey would probably want to help. He kicks a lot of ass these days, almost as much as my mom."

Izzie looked impressed. "If we could actually gather all those people, we would have a ridiculous strike team. The combined power of our families alone is massive. I have a few people I've met throughout the years, and a lot of them have suffered at the hands of the dark wizards." She nodded a few times and anticipation crept onto her face. "The light families versus the dark families."

"I always figured the Brownstone family was more gray than light." Alison raised her teacup and took a sip.

"I can work with that." The other woman took a few deep breaths. "I've wanted to ask you. How is he doing?"

"Who?"

"Luke. I read all about it." Izzie ran her hand through her hair. "He's another thing I think about when I wonder how things could have been different. When I first went on the run, I used to think it wouldn't be for that long. That we'd smash the dark families hunting us within a few months or something."

"He's doing well," Alison replied softly. "He misses you. He's not with anyone else, you know. I think, on some level, he's waiting for you."

Izzie let out a bitter laugh. "That's exactly like him. The loyal wolf to the end, huh?"

"Why don't you ever see him?"

"Because of shit like what happened in D.C." She curled her fingers into a fist and slowly opened them. "The only thing that has kept him safe is that I've stayed away from him. I've stayed away from everyone except you, if only because I knew you could handle anyone who might come after you. I didn't want to give those bastards anyone to target because I knew that if I did, innocent people would suffer."

"You said it yourself. You now have forward movement." Alison set her tea down and poured herself some sake. A little buzz didn't sound so bad anymore. "If you've found this much, then you're close. No. We're close. We only need a few more pieces of information and we can take the fight to them—and you can have your life back." She poured a cup of sake for her friend. "How about a toast?"

"To what?"

Alison picked up her cup. "To kicking dark wizard ass."

"Even if it won't happen right away?"

"Better late than never." Alison grinned.

"To kicking dark wizard ass," Izzie intoned.

CHAPTER THIRTEEN

A few days later, Alison stepped into the conference room. Whether or not they were close to ending the dark wizard threat hanging over both of them, she still had a company to run. Until she or Izzie had something more concrete to work with, that's what Alison would continue to do.

Is this obsession? Even if I can ignore them for a few days or weeks? I wonder if Mason went looking for a big job because I told him I met with Izzie.

Hana, Mason, Tahir, and Ava already sat at the conference room table. Alison headed over to her chair. "Okay, everyone's here." She nodded to Mason. "You said you had a possible big job but it couldn't involve the field support team."

He nodded. "I'll explain why in a minute, but it will require an all-magical team. That's non-negotiable, even if the client isn't a magical. That's why I didn't ask Jerry to come to the meeting."

Ava tapped a few notes into her tablet but didn't say anything.

"Who's the client?" Alison asked.

"Abigail Wilson, the CEO of Aeternum," Mason stated.

"Aeternum." Alison frowned as she tossed the name around in her mind. There was nothing more frustrating than *almost* remembering something. "What do they do?"

Tahir cleared his throat. He never missed an opportunity to explain something when presented with one. "They specialize in the extraction and refining of terrestrial magical ingredients to supply industrial customers, particularly the technomagic companies. Even if they can't provide everything that direct import from Oriceran can, they can often provide suitable substitutes. It's far easier for most other companies to deal with an American company than it is with some of the various groups and organizations on Oriceran."

The life wizard nodded. "Exactly. I did a few months of security work for Abigail a few years back when New Veil made some threats against her. She's a tough woman but honest, and she contacted me directly this morning about hiring Brownstone Security as a special security team on a business trip. Her security is going through some reorganization right now, and most of them are non-magicals."

"Why does she need an all-magical team?" Hana asked, her brow furrowed. "Give a couple of guys power armor and anti-magic bullets, and they can fight a magical. Rich people can afford that kind of protection."

"It's about where the business trip is." Mason nodded to Ava.

She tapped a few times on her tablet. A three-dimensional holographic image of the globe appeared above the conference table and spun until it was centered on the Atlantic Ocean. It zoomed in to a small mountainous island covered in dense forest.

He pointed to the globe. "That is Nereid Island."

"Nereid Island?" Alison echoed. "As in the sea nymphs from Greek mythology?"

"It turns out the legends were inspired by actual Oricerans who came over the last time the gates were open," he explained. "Long-lived sea-linked humanoid females. They're an all-female population really sensitive to background magic energy. The island happens to be directly above heavy deposits of a rare form of aventurine that is good at absorbing magical energy. Even when the gates closed, there was a massive amount of residual energy in the aventurine. The Nereids could only survive on the island on Earth because of that. It's much like a super-kemana, but they also used the magical energy to conceal the island. I don't know all the details, but something about the time they've spent on Earth means they can't really go back to Oriceran, either. They still use the high levels of magic to keep the island defended from outsiders, and they've managed to maintain their independence despite a small population. They're building their wealth up by allowing small amounts of aventurine mining."

"And small population means what, exactly?" Alison asked.

"We're talking only dozens of them. From what I understand, when one dies, that somehow frees up energy for a new one to be born, but most of what I know I learned from Abigail in a phone call this morning." Mason shrugged, an apologetic look on his face.

"I wondered how that worked on an island of all females," Hana remarked with a snicker. "And fancy, a hidden magical island. That's cool even by our standards."

Alison nodded as she absorbed all the information. Even as a powerful Drow princess, there were so many things she didn't know about her own planet. "I take it that Abigail wants to establish some sort of mining deal with the Nereids?"

"Exactly," he confirmed. "They had trouble with the last company and are looking for new partners. They're still very leery of the outside world and have now confined themselves to companies headed by females because they're already distrustful of males. They also don't trust non-magicals in general."

"But Abigail isn't a magical."

"Apparently, she had some positive interaction with them in the past when she previously tried to negotiate a deal," he explained. "Abigail also feels they'll tolerate Brownstone Security sending a team that includes men because a woman leads the company. We won't be able to get any signal from the island, and spells will have trouble breaking through their barriers, so I thought a small team — me, Hana, and you, A." He looked at Tahir. "No offense. I merely think this won't be a situation that plays to your strengths."

The infomancer didn't appear fazed by the exclusion. "Ignoring that, you three still represent a significant show of force. Does Miss Wilson fear imminent attack?"

Mason sighed. "She's spooked after the Friends of

Carlyle attack, along with a few other HDL militant and New Veil attacks in recent months. You have to understand that the New Veil came close to killing her the last time. A sniper lined up on her and fired a shot. I barely managed to jump in front of her in time." He slapped his chest. "If that asshole had used anti-magics, I'd probably be dead, and there was a good chance that bullet would have gone through and taken her out, too."

Hana whistled. "Damn, Mason. That's some solid body-guarding."

Even Tahir looked impressed. Alison smiled, proud of him even if she hadn't known him then.

"If we're talking about a remote island with a heavy magical barrier, I'm not worried about New Veil snipers," she said after a moment's thought. "Tahir and Sonya can support Jerry and the field support personnel while they work local jobs." She pondered the possible dangers. "That said, it'd be nice if we had at least one more field witch." She gave Hana a meaningful look.

The other woman nodded back.

"I don't disagree," Mason replied, "but who did you have in mind?"

Ava looked at Alison, cold curiosity in her stern gaze.

"If Drysi Jones is still in town, I might try to persuade her to come along. It'll be a nice little test to see how she works with the team. And it might convince her to join us." She shrugged. "Maybe we don't need her for this job, but it wouldn't hurt."

The faint tension seeped from Ava's face. "It might be best to test her compatibility further in a situation that doesn't present immediate and intense personal risk."

"That sounds good to me." Hana gave a thumbs-up.

Tahir shrugged, clearly disinterested in the field personnel decision.

Mason nodded. "I've heard enough about her to believe she'll be a help, but are you sure she'll come?"

"The worst thing that happens is she says no," Alison replied. She smiled, feeling good about the choice. After the conversations she'd had with the witch, she was convinced she'd make a good addition to the team.

CHAPTER FOURTEEN

Mason eyed Alison from across their cozy corner table at the Forbidden Bean. She'd suggested that they experiment with afternoon coffee at the shop when they weren't working a job. This was despite them having great coffee machines and beans in the breakrooms and offices in the Brownstone Building.

She had authorized Ava to employ "all necessary means" to ensure "coffee satisfaction" among staff. Compared to the cost of anti-magic deflectors and anti-magic bullets, the price of a few extra bags of premium coffee was little more than a rounding error.

He wasn't all that interested in leaving the building during the day when they already had access to perfectly good coffee, but a smart man picked his battles. Challenging his girlfriend-boss over her preference of coffee location seemed like a battle that would earn him nothing but enmity, even if he won.

Alison sat there with a slight frown on her face as she

stared at her cup as if she tried to will it to swirl with some previously hidden Drow magical control technique.

She'd been quieter than normal, and although Mason had theories over the reason, he couldn't be sure.

This is the problem with Hana not living with her anymore, he thought. *No one's there to pull her back to Earth a lot of the time. She sits at home at night and worries too much. Like she has to be the one to solve every problem in Seattle—or, shit, the country.*

It's not like Alison can have heart-to-hearts with Sonya about what it means to be Alison Brownstone, Drow Princess and daughter of James Brownstone.

I wish I could convince her to move in with me. Then again, maybe she simply hates the coffee today and I'm the one over-thinking this.

"Is something wrong?" he asked softly. "Too bitter? You seem to be hating on the milk and sugar a lot lately."

"Blacker coffee wakes me up better, and I know that coffee won't have any weird side effects like drinking too many energy potions. That was a wild weekend." She shuddered and looked up from her cup with an uncertain expression. "Why did you even ask that? Was I making a weird face or something?" She sounded curious, not offended.

Mason nodded. "Sure, we'll go with *or something.*"

"Very diplomatic." She shook her head. "The coffee's fine. I was thinking about some other things that have been on my mind lately."

"Other things? What other things? Are you still upset about Myna?"

"Not exactly. But I have wondered if all this stuff with

dark wizards is justified or if I'm...I don't know, dangerously obsessed." Alison shrugged. "It's not something I worried about before, but it's definitely been on my mind more often these days."

Nope. I was right to worry. It's time to steer the SS Brownstone away from the Reef of Unnecessary Martyrdom.

"Obsessed?" Mason set his cup down. "One thing to keep in mind, A, is that all our jobs lately have had nothing to do with dark wizards, and this Nereid thing coming up doesn't either. It's hard for you to be obsessed if you spend most of your time not doing anything to dark wizards. At the other times when you were involved, someone else pushed you into it. If anything, they're obsessed with you and Seattle, not the other way around."

She frowned as if not entirely convinced. "I get that, but it's not always about what you do. It's about what you think about. They've set up house in my mind, and I don't even make them pay rent." She forced a chuckle, but her grim expression barely changed.

"That's why you think you're obsessed? Because you think about dark wizards too much?"

I thought all that stiffness the last few days was because of Myna. I don't know if this is better or worse.

Alison looked uneasy. "Maybe? I do think about them all the time. Even before Izzie stopped by and we tried to put together an ass-kicking roster, I've been pissed about them. This goes all the way back to my time on Oriceran, and the more I think about it, the more I wonder. Do you know why I went to Oriceran?"

"Sure," he replied and tried to keep a smile on his face despite some building confusion. "You went there because you figured the Drow would help you better understand your shadow magic. That's what you told me before. You avoided them for a long time because of what went down between the queen and your dad and finally decided it was time."

"That's true, but it's not the whole story." She raised her hand and a purple-black orb coalesced in the palm. "My heritage means I have access to more types of magic than a pure Drow, but during my time at the School of Necessary Magic, most of what they taught me applied more to light magic, not my Drow shadow magic." She raised her hand and the orb grew larger. Thankfully, they were tucked into a rear corner table and Mason's broad shoulders blocked her from the customers' view so they wouldn't be alarmed. "I didn't feel strong enough to do what I needed to do with only that training, as good as it was. I wanted and *needed* the Drow to help me become stronger. Of course, when I told them that, they ate that up."

Mason nodded slowly. "There's nothing wrong with wanting to strengthen your magic. I've trained my magic my entire life, and it's not because I wanted revenge against dark wizards."

Alison tossed the orb between her hands and earned a curious look from the barista across the room who simply shrugged and turned away. "They were suspicious of me, but they still wanted to help. They thought it was merely my Drow nature that wanted to be strong to defeat enemies, but I had specific enemies in mind. Every time I trained with the Drow, I thought about how I needed to gain power so no one I cared about would get hurt by a dark wizard ever again." She crushed the orb in her hand

and it disappeared. "I need power to be able to do that. I need to be the strongest. Maybe even stronger than my dad."

"It's not wrong to want to protect the people you care about, A." He chuckled. "I've been a bodyguard my whole life. My whole deal is to protect people. I don't have a problem if you want to do that."

"Thanks, but I'm not sure it helps." She returned to her fixed stare into the dark coffee. "I constantly tell myself it's justified, that I need to be the person to protect everyone, but then I wonder about Myna."

"I thought you said she wasn't the reason for this." Mason's face scrunched up in confusion. "And what does she have to do with dark wizards? I thought she hadn't even been to Earth for hundreds of years. Did she have some dealings with them in the past?"

Alison shook her head. "No. She has nothing to do with the dark wizards. It's her sacrifice that gets to me."

"That I already knew."

"Yeah, I know I'm not always that mysterious." She frowned. "She's convinced I'm part of some big future plans for the Drow and she was justified in doing something incredibly dangerous because of that." She glanced out the window at a passing car. "I'd tried to tell her before that I'm not that important, but I've practically planned to take the dark families on myself. When I think about that, it's like I've bought into her destiny shit but in a different way."

I need to stop her before she lets this eat her alive.

"Wait a sec, A," Mason began. He lowered his voice after a quick glance around the almost empty coffee shop. "I get where you're coming from, but this isn't you looking for a fight that wouldn't otherwise come. The dark wizards have targeted you and your friends many times, all the way back to the events at the school. Yes, it might not be that you're the only person on the planet who can stop them, but if the dark wizards want to mess with you, there's nothing wrong with repaying them. That's not obsession. It's self-defense, and every one of them you eliminate is one less threat in the future."

Alison lifted her cup and took a sip. She nodded. "Sometimes, the best defense is a good offense? It is the Brownstone family way."

"A little offense never hurts." He pointed to his chest. "And remember, this isn't only about you anymore. Not only did we have to deal with them on a job, they attacked Brownstone Security directly. They could have killed any of us." He shook his head. "Call it obsession if you want to, but I'd like a little payback myself. Not only because they attacked me, but because those fuckers have targeted my girlfriend. No man worthy to be called a man wants to stand by and let people try to hurt the woman he loves."

Her face softened. "But stopping them doesn't mean someone else won't come after us in the future. My dad had to go through a lot of bodies before people finally bought a damned clue."

Mason grunted. Given the public exploits of James Brownstone he'd heard about, that was surprising, but the bodyguard had dealt with his own share of stubborn assassins, thugs, and criminals. Strength attracted strength, both positive and negative.

"But they did eventually figure it out," he pointed out.

"And the Brownstone Effect in Seattle proves that people are starting to figure it out for you, too." He gestured around the coffee shop. "A place like this would have never opened before you set up shop here. It's not like new gangs constantly show up to take over because you eliminated the old ones."

Alison laughed quietly. "You're saying expensive but delicious coffee is proof that people are learning not to mess with me?"

"Exactly." He grinned.

"I should tell the police to stop bothering with crime statistics and look at coffee shops."

"Maybe you should." His grin faded as he locked eyes with his girlfriend. "Always remember, A, it's not only your family who has your back. I have your back. Hana has your back. Tahir, Ava—everyone. We're all invested in all of this, not only the dark wizards. If the weight of the world is heavy on your shoulders, share it with your friends."

Alison looked thoughtful and nodded. "I get that. Trust me, I do. But this stuff with Myna made me think about the people around me and the price they might have to pay if I don't make sure they're safe."

Mason raised an eyebrow. "Do you actually understand? I'll bet that in the back of your mind, you're still trying to see how you can solve everything yourself. You all but said so. You need to dial down the *noblesse oblige*, princess. We commoners are fairly good at defending ourselves."

Two women several tables away glanced at them and murmured under their breaths. Mason and Alison were speaking quietly, but their body language signaled tension to the rest of the room.

Alison scoffed. "That's not what this is. The only reason being a Drow princess is important is because it comes with significant magical power. I have a responsibility to use that power to help people."

"You don't have a responsibility to get yourself killed in the process." His face tightened. He loved her too much to let her return to that kind of thinking. "I get it. I know who your parents are. I understand the kind of things you went through when you were at the School of Necessary Magic." He took a deep breath and held his hand up. "I'm not saying you have to stand back and let dark wizards or anyone else push you around. I'm merely saying that when the time comes and you need to kick a castle door down, bring a fucking army with you, and we'll annihilate those bastards together. That's what friends are for, whether you date them or not."

She leaned back in her seat, her gaze distant and lost for a long, silent moment. Finally, she released a small chuckle. "Okay, point taken. You win."

"Really? I should record you saying that."

"Keep talking, and you'll lose." She laughed and shook her head. "It's a good thing I started the company. If I didn't have you all around to pull me back to Earth, who knows what might have happened?"

Yes, what would have?

CHAPTER FIFTEEN

Alison stifled a yawn as she pulled her Fiat Spider out of the Brownstone Building garage and onto the street. Her team had spent the day training and on standby. Jerry's team hadn't needed any help on their low-key job to escort some corporate executives to and from a meeting on Mercer Island.

I act like crazy shit happens every day, but it doesn't. Sure, dangerous and weird stuff happens to me more often than to a lot of people, but I have plenty of downtime. I have to remember that and not always see a dark wizard hiding behind every trash can or delivery drone.

She still hadn't fully adjusted to the idea that her company made money even when she wasn't directly involved. Not being a control freak helped, but it remained weird to receive a call or text and realize she had earned a fat paycheck for sending someone else to do something.

Heavy is the crown there, princess.

Alison chuckled.

For now, though, the upcoming Nereid job would

require the Dark Princess and her courtiers, not Jerry and his non-magical team. Ava and Mason had already worked out the practical travel arrangements with Abigail.

They'd use one of her corporate jets and the CEO client was comfortable that the Brownstone team thoroughly inspect the plane before they took off. The pilot was a man who had worked for Abigail for years, and Ava and Tahir had already performed a background check and found nothing questionable.

I let my first few months of jobs throw off my sense of expectation. Most jobs don't end in some big showdown, especially if people know I'm involved. Sometimes, it's merely a matter of a show of force.

There was one last matter she needed to clear up before they left in a couple of days.

After she'd turned at an intersection, she set her phone to speaker mode and dialed Drysi Jones. Tahir had done a deep background check on the witch and everything matched up with the few scraps Alison had learned from the other woman.

The Jones family's once impressive wealth was long gone, and Drysi had scraped by as a bounty hunter. The real surprise was that her money troubles weren't because she didn't score impressive bounties. From what they could tell, it was because she gave large amounts of her money away after she'd earned it.

Alison was concerned at first and wondered if Drysi was being blackmailed. Tahir's investigation established that the people who received money were all members of families who used to work for the Jones family but were now in financial distress. It was an actual example of *noblesse oblige*.

Mason thought Alison had the world on her shoulders, but it wasn't like she gave all her money to old Drow servants.

No. Merely her diseases.

Damn it. That was Myna's choice, and I'll respect that. The only thing left is to move forward.

She cleared her throat as she waited for the call to connect.

"I won't lie. I didn't expect a call from the Dark Princess so soon." Drysi answered with slight amusement in her voice. "I'm not complaining. I'm simply surprised."

Alison chuckled. "First of all, are you still in town? If you're not, that doesn't change things. It merely means we might have to work out a few transportation issues concerning an offer I want to make."

"Yes, I'm still in town. I planned to leave in a few days and head back to Cardiff. Why? What offer are you talking about?"

"I have a job coming up," she explained. "It's an unusual one and I could use another magical watching my back."

"That sounds interesting, if somewhat generic," the woman replied. "Would you care to be a little more specific?"

"We can meet somewhere to discuss it in person," Alison suggested. "No offense, Drysi, but I can't give you too many details until I know you'll do the job, and I also don't want to discuss too much over the phone. I can say it involves a little international travel and for various reasons, I can't bring along most of my team, including all my non-magicals. If you don't have a big bounty to track, it'd be nice to have you on board. If it helps, I don't think it'll be a dangerous job, so it'll effectively be a free vacation." She chuckled. "Better than that, actually. It's not only a free vacation but one you'll be paid for. I'll pay well, and I know you might not be interested in joining Team Brownstone yet, but you might change your mind after you spend a few days with us."

Drysi laughed. "Pretty confident, aren't we?"

"I'd like to think we're a roguishly lovable bunch."

"I could see myself working with a group like that."

"And to be clear, this won't involve dark wizards or traffickers," Alison explained. "It's a corporate escort job but to an unusual place. We vet our clients, though, and I don't take on any whom I can't stand behind, especially after all that crap with Scott Carlyle."

"A right bloody bastard that one. It's a good time to consider joining your company since you don't have any billionaires gunning for you."

She laughed. "Exactly. So, you interested in talking about the job?"

Drysi snickered quietly. "The mysterious escort job to an *unusual* place. All right, Alison. Name a place and we'll meet to discuss the job. It wouldn't hurt me to listen, but I'll make you pay."

"No problem." She glanced at the console clock. "How about Maneki? It's a sushi place not that far from Pioneer Square. Maybe two hours?"

"That's fine. I'll look it up and I'll see you then."

"See you."

The witch ended the call.

Alison smiled and satisfaction filled her. Getting Drysi to meet with her was eighty percent of the challenge in her mind. The kind of woman who donated most of her own money to help other people was the kind of woman Alison could use in Brownstone Security.

She's helped me fight dark wizards and traffickers. I can use that kind of integrity.

Drysi sighed as she leaned up against her hotel room door, a communication crystal in her hand. She and Alison had shared a pleasant meal together where they discussed the straight-forward job. Playing coy about joining Brownstone Security had worked as well as Conrad had predicted.

I merely need to finish the job, she thought wearily. *Everything will be better then. It's for the best that she's taken out of the picture. No individual should be that disruptive.*

The witch ran her free hand through her hair. Helping assassinate Alison wasn't anything personal, but it'd be easier to feel better about the job if the damned woman had been more what she'd expected—an entitled, arrogant Drow with little concern other than to display her power over others.

Alison saved my life in DC, and Conrad didn't give two shits that I almost died. I'm nothing but a tool to him.

The bounty hunter fisted her hands, her jaw tight. It didn't matter what Conrad felt about her. She was using him as much as he used her.

Alison wanted her for the team, but there was no

hidden agenda and the woman seemed to care about her subordinates. She already seemed to care about Drysi and they barely knew each other.

Damn it. Conrad was right. Now, Alison wants me for her company more than ever, which means her guard will be down. Even if it is better for me, I hate the idea of that bloody bastard's scheme working out the way he said it would.

She patted a small pendant that hung underneath her shirt, a truth-bender loaned to her by Conrad. She'd been convinced she would need it, that the paranoid Dark Princess would want to test her loyalty through magic exactly as Conrad had when he first approached her.

She believes me, and all I had to do was nearly die several times in front of her.

Drysi's laugh was dark and bitter. She had to do this. The Jones name was dwindling to nothing—less than nothing.

Conrad might be a venomous snake but he had offered her a way to bring back her family's glory. She could earn the money but without the status, it was useless. He wasn't even wrong about why the dark families needed to gain control.

The fact that bounty hunters and people like Alison had to stop trouble proved how out-of-control the world had become. If the governments couldn't keep things in check, the dark families would. It was so obvious.

Yes, some innocent people have been hurt, but we'll help more people more in the long run. Even Conrad will. It doesn't matter what motivates him. It only matters what happens in the end.

Drysi raised the crystal and spoke the activation incantation.

"Report," Conrad barked over the magical communication link.

"Everything's gone even better than you planned. She's invited me along on a job and I've accepted. I think me turning her down before has left her with even more reason to be nice and trusting."

"Of course. We've underestimated Alison Brownstone for too long. We thought she was more like her adopted father or a pure Drow—easy to maneuver and deal with accordingly." Conrad sighed. "Failure because of ignorance is shameful, but we've learned from our mistakes. I take it you baited her successfully?"

"Nice and tidy this time, for sure," the witch replied and her voice wavered slightly. "I even let myself almost be killed by some bloody garbage wizard not worthy of the name."

"Your commitment to the cause will be rewarded. And, yes, you're right. So many witches and wizards aren't worthy of their powers. This situation—no, this world—is wrong. I know some of what we've asked has puzzled and challenged you at times but sacrifice for the greater good always seems painful when you lack a full understanding of the big picture."

Drysi scoffed. She stepped away from the door and sat on the edge of the bed. "Why don't you let me in on the big picture?"

"Don't be foolish, Miss Jones." Conrad released a pained sigh. "Despite our setbacks at the hands of Brownstone, Berens, and others, our operations still proceed because those in the field only have the information they need for their individual missions. Your successful manipulation of

Brownstone and the truth-bender aren't enough to guarantee that you won't be discovered and interrogated. But enough with that. Tell me about this job."

She relayed the details of the Aeternum job.

"How utterly perfect." He laughed. "I'd go so far as to say the universe has asked us to destroy Alison Brownstone on this island. If she dies there, we will have no PDA and no James Brownstone to storm into the area and demand answers. It doesn't even matter whether her little friends survive or not. Not only that, if you can also disrupt the meeting of this Wilson woman with the Nereids, I can have a female representative contact the island and we can set up our own aventurine agreement."

"That's what I thought." Drysi ran her tongue along the inside of her mouth as she considered the options. "It'd be easy enough to plant something about New Veil, too, or the Friends of Carlyle. She'll be on an island surrounded by magic. It'll be harder to realize what I might be up to."

"Excellent, Miss Jones." Conrad sniffed, a hint of disdain in it. "This will help make up for your failures in DC."

"My failures?" The witch scoffed. "How are those my failures? All your other little pawns and plans didn't work out and it's my fault?"

"Watch your tone, Miss Jones," he reprimanded sharply. "Until you've completed your assigned task, you're in no position to question me or my leadership. My family, unlike yours, doesn't lie in ruins because of their failures and lack of vision."

She ground her teeth. "I have only one question for you."

"And what might that be?"

"The wizard you had me eliminate—the bait for Alison." She took a deep breath. "You said you'd worked with him in the past."

"He'd supplied some of my people through indirect channels. I had never dealt with him directly. Why? He's dead now, and I already made it clear that was acceptable and preferred. What does it matter?"

"Were you aware that he was involved in trafficking women?" Drysi asked, her voice cold.

Conrad sighed. "Miss Jones, when we're forced to move in the shadows, we will occasionally find ourselves beside roaches. You again fail to understand the big picture."

"And what is that in this case?"

"That man was a symptom of a world out of balance, a world not under proper control," he explained. "Once the proper order is established—our order—all such problems will be rectified. In the meantime, however, limits on resources mean that not every social ill can be fixed, and on occasion, that means the sacrifices of innocents are necessary."

Drysi frowned and her fingers tightened around the communications crystal. "You make it sound so trivial and not the bloody travesty it is."

He snorted. "Oh, please, Miss Jones. You've killed for the cause in the past, including people who weren't a direct threat. Now, you worry about a few non-magical lives lost along the way? A little suffering? It's too late to care now. There's blood on your hands. But if you think you can't do it, fine. We can assign the task to someone else and we'll both know exactly what the Jones family name means."

Her jaw tightened. She wished the crystal would allow him to see her face.

Bloody bastard. I hope that someday, he ends up in a room with Brownstone.

Drysi took several deep breaths. No. Conrad would never end up in a room with Brownstone because the Welsh witch would kill her very soon.

"I'll handle Brownstone and I'll make sure Wilson doesn't get her deal," she replied, her voice almost a whisper. "I'll show you what being a Jones means."

"Yes, the blood will tell. It always does. Don't contact me again until after Brownstone's dead."

"Fine."

It's worth it. Once I remove her, it'll all be worth it.

CHAPTER SIXTEEN

Tahir watched a small drone zoom under a ramp in the tactical training room. The machine tried to escape a simulated baby silver dragon only a few yards in length. The drone cut to the side and avoided a narrow blast of ice breath. Follow-up wobbles saved it from the next two ice attacks.

Sonya sat beside him and sweat beaded on her forehead. She wore a haptic interface glove on her right hand, her wand snapped into a center groove. A small pair of thick opaque goggles were strapped over her eyes, her own custom AR and VR combination she'd created with his assistance.

She's improved far more rapidly than even I anticipated. If she'd received decent training to begin with, she could already be a true force. Alas.

The drone dropped and skimmed over a walkway. The angry flying reptile continued in pursuit and roared defiance, loud despite its modest size. Sonya trembled slightly at the noise.

This is good. Exposure will allow her to better cope with such problems more effectively in the future. After the Fremont Troll incident, who knows what we might end up having to deal with?

"In this case, since you're using a magical link, you need to take better advantage of that," Tahir explained. "It'll help you improve your fundamental reaction time. Speed wins. Slowness kills. Of course, there are other ways to improve reaction time, some of which involve not using magic, but we'll discuss that in a moment."

Sonya gritted her teeth and twisted her arm. The drone looped around a walkway and the pursuing dragon slammed into the hard wood and metal with a yelp. It faded from existence a few seconds later.

He rubbed his chin as he finished his evaluation of his apprentice's performance.

She took a few deep breaths and raised her goggles. "Shouldn't I train against things we'll actually run into? I don't think I've ever heard about a dragon in Seattle."

"I'm sure one of the many foes Alison has run into said at one point, 'What are the chances that I'll run into a Drow princess who can fly?' Proper preparation can overcome differentials in strength."

The girl smirked. "You got me, man. So how do you think I did? Only *adequate* like last time?"

The infomancer opened his mouth but didn't respond immediately. He had planned to tell the girl she'd done an adequate job, but Hana constantly chided him for being rude.

If I didn't respect the girl's talent, I wouldn't have agreed to train her, but no one else seems to understand that, even the girl herself. Ah, it's so difficult when people want to substitute social niceties for efficient honesty.

"You did a good job," he said testily. "I don't force these types of practices for amusement but to further open your mind. You can even think of it as an attempt to force a paradigm change."

"A paradigm change?" Sonya frowned and shook out her gloved hand. "Huh? You never mentioned that before."

"I'm a firm believer that you need to have a certain amount of experience with something before you can even begin to attempt to understand it. As you're not teaching yourself anymore, you can follow my lead even without knowing the ultimate destination."

Sonya gave him a slight nod but her scrunched expression suggested that she didn't understand. "What does that have to do with that paradigm change stuff?"

"If you think too much like a normal witch, you won't maximize your particular advantages. Of course, any wizard or witch can, with enough practice, theoretically duplicate the abilities of any other, but specialization allows for greater feats in specific contexts. As infomancers, we also trade some initial flexibility for greater power in our specialization. But to truly make use of that, you have to think appropriately. That's what I mean by paradigm change. But a demonstration will help make it particularly clear." Tahir gestured to the drone. "Shield it."

Sonya raised her gloved hand with the wand and whispered an incantation. A shimmering shield appeared around the mechanical.

He narrowed his eyes. "Adequate. And you're still able to move it?"

She moved her arm a few times, and the small drone flew back and forth for several yards with little trouble.

Her instructor raised his wand and his phone. He gestured with the wand and pressed a button on his device to access a file that stored glyphs. Power was power, no matter how it was contained.

The rotors of the drone cut out and the poor device tumbled instantly. Sonya's eyes widened as it crashed into the hard ground and pieces erupted with a violent crack.

Tahir stuck his wand and phone in his back pocket and nodded, satisfied that the level of destruction provided an appropriate illustration of his intended lesson.

"What the hell, man?" the girl yelled. "That's not cool."

He shrugged, his face a cool mask. "As I said, paradigm. Even Alison would focus on how to destroy the drone with brute force. You should have anticipated that I might piggyback off your own control link and make allowance for it. Even if I were able to break through your defenses, it would have been a challenge and you would have been able to save the drone. Just because you're not in your preferred environment doesn't mean you should let your guard down." He sighed. "Where is the confident girl who defeated Hana despite all the tricks she played?"

Sonya sighed and looked down. "Sorry. I know I suck compared to you."

"My experience is greater than yours, but that's not what I want you to focus on. Don't look down."

"Huh?"

"Look at me," he commanded, his tone sharp.

Sonya raised her head but looked to the side.

Tahir walked right in front of her. "You need to realize one very important thing."

"Yeah, yeah. I know. I know. Paradigm. Change my mind." She gave him a little salute but she did manage to look directly at him. "I'll do better next time. I let my guard down because of where we were. I get it. I screwed up." She shrugged. "You beat me."

Tahir shook his head. "That's not what I'm talking about. Not at all."

"Then what are you talking about?"

He stepped back. "Your parents were myopic trash. You're far better off away from them. You were even better off away from them before you met us."

The girl laughed. "I can't disagree. I've thought about tracking them down to rub it in their faces that I work for Alison, but I thought that would only cause trouble."

"You still miss the importance of what I'm getting at, but I admit I'm less than efficient at getting my point across." The infomancer frowned. "While your natural talent for infomancy is very high, you lack universal confidence. This is another cage for your mind. A fear of failures or a fear of others means valuable mental energy is consumed by self-doubt. I hoped that simply training you these last few months would eliminate that, and while you're confident enough when you don't have to be around your target, that glorious confidence fades if you share a room with others. It's a fundamental weakness."

"I'm confident enough," Sonya countered. She flourished her wand. "At least when it comes to infomancy. But it's hard for me to look at people and be around them. It makes me nervous. What can I say?"

"It makes you nervous only because your wastrel parents neglected and abused you." Tahir glowered, angrier than he'd expected. "If you're confident in one area, then you should allow that confidence to flow into all areas of your life and improvement will naturally follow."

"That's easy for you to say. You're already a fully trained wizard. You're so good at it, the Dark Princess came looking for you."

He shook his head. "There's always someone stronger or better. Admittedly, not many in my case, but that's irrelevant. For example, I communicate and engage on equal terms with Alison, even though her absolute level of magical power is far superior to mine. Acknowledging that differential doesn't mean I disavow my own worth, as I have my own skills and advantages over her. You will never reach your full potential until you accept that you're worthy of it and the respect of others." He chuckled. "Hana and Alison mean well, but I think they're wrong. You wouldn't be afraid of others if you respected yourself more, and I think you need to be taught a kind of purposeful arrogance."

Sonya tucked her hands into the pockets of her hoodie. "Purposeful arrogance? What's that?"

"Arrogance can be a tool—a weapon—if wielded properly to inspire oneself and not to delude. Perhaps arrogance is too extreme a way to describe it rather than supreme confidence, but the truth is still important regardless of how you articulate the concept."

"The truth?"

"Yes," Tahir replied. "Always remember, Sonya. If you

must lie, lie to others but never lie to yourself. Know your limits but acknowledge your skills."

She smirked. "Hana will be pissed when I tell her you said I need to be even cockier—and all the time."

He tilted his chin, a slight smirk on his face. "My confidence is one of the reasons she's attracted to me."

The girl rolled her eyes. "Okay, I get it. You're a total badass in every way."

"No, you don't get it. My point is that *you* need to believe that as well and not only when you're safely ensconced at your workstation." He gestured around the room. "You need true bravery, and I intend to grow that in you. It's my challenge, and I don't lose at challenges."

Sonya blinked several times and dropped her head, a light blush on her face.

"Take some time to think on it. I'm reasonable and I don't expect things to change quickly." He strolled toward the drone wreckage. "But to be clear, you're not upset about not going to the island, are you?"

"No way, man." She fell in beside him. "That would be way too stressful, and from what Mason said, it sounds all boring and low-tech there."

"Boring is relative, but I'm glad you're not displeased. Frankly, I'm glad I won't go simply because I dislike travel." Tahir stopped and knelt to pick up a small piece of a rotor blade. "There's something else I've thought about. A way to address some of my training concerns and also some of Hana and Alison's concerns about your socialization. I'll acknowledge that if you perhaps had more practice in those skills it would benefit your purposeful arrogance as well."

Sonya gathered the smaller drone pieces. "I won't go to some magical boarding school. Screw that. If you guys try to send me, I'll run off to Laramie or something."

"Laramie?" The infomancer raised a questioning brow.

"It's the first place I thought of." She shrugged.

"I see." He nodded. "No, we won't send you to a magic school. The key is paradigm, and it extends beyond magic. It's a way to understand and interact with the world." He picked up the main cracked body of the small drone. "Do you know the major advantage Earth magicals have over Oriceran magicals?"

She frowned and shook her head.

"Ours is a civilization with thousands of years of advancements that aren't dependent on magic," he explained. "This is why most of the technomagic advancements come from this side of the gates, even if the occasional Oriceran discovers something interesting. Oricerans have a locked paradigm of their own. They are too used to using magic for everything. On Earth, even the mightiest wizard recognizes the value of technology."

"That's cool and all, man, but what's that got to do with me?"

Tahir turned the drone body over a few times as he examined the damage. "Because of the dark wizard attack, you experienced a true battle. We had many advantages going into that fight, but we can't always depend on such things. We need to make sure we have advantages that we carry with us wherever we go and regardless of whether we have a comfortable workstation to hide in or not."

"Wherever we go? You mean like an expanding haptic glove?" Sonya's face twisted in deep thought. "I've tried to practice with the stored spells, but I still have trouble keeping them from messing up."

"I applaud your initiative, but that's not what I mean." He shook his head. "I mean non-magical skills. The more things you can do without magic, the better. Neither of us is Alison. The level of raw power we have is limited, which means the more we try to do with magic, the less effective we'll be. You should reserve magic for situations where it'll provide a key critical advantage and instead, use other skills whenever possible."

Sonya inspected a drone shard for a few seconds before she responded. "That makes sense, but what does that actually mean? As in…like, what do I do?"

"It means many things." The infomancer frowned in thought. "For one thing, your personal fitness needs to improve. The facilities we have here are more than sufficient to achieve that."

The girl laughed. "You want me to start going to PE?"

"Effectively, yes. A fit body leads to a fit mind, and to be blunt, you never know when you might need to run for your life, even if you don't work for a security company. The people living near the Fremont Troll learned that lesson firsthand."

She swallowed and nodded.

"Second, the more non-magical techniques you can employ, regardless of the task, the more useful your magic will be overall. You'll add to something that is already good, rather than try to create it, to begin with." He shook the drone body. "When we had our race when we first met, as it were, you used a lot of magic."

"So?" She averted her eyes once again, a light blush on her face.

"One of the reasons you could do that was because you already had good control." Tahir tucked the drone piece under his arm. "And that got me thinking. I've looked around and there are many youth-oriented drone battle racing leagues. Most have strict rules about using magic. I think it'd be a useful exercise for you to participate in those."

Sonya blinked a few times. "You want me to join some junior drone battle league? Seriously?"

He nodded. "Yes, seriously. You'll learn to better hone your drone piloting skills without relying primarily on your magic for the flight itself, which means you'll instinctively save your magic for when it'll be most useful. In addition, you'll also have a chance to socialize with like-minded individuals around your age who are less likely to be complete fools, if only because of their interest in the sport."

She immediately gave him her defiant teenager eye-roll. "Huh. Really selling the fun, aren't you, man?"

"You should find enjoyment where you can, but I won't force you to do anything. As in everything since I've started to train you, I offer you resources and paths to self-improvement. But in the end, you have to choose them." He shrugged. "If you trust me, you'll listen to me."

Sonya took a deep breath and bit her lip. "It does sound kind of fun." Her eyes filled with genuine warmth. "And thanks. I know I can be a pain and a bitch."

Tahir offered her a thin smile. "I wouldn't waste my time if you weren't worth the effort."

As the girl returned his smile, he was struck by something rare for him—complete surprise. Even though he'd recognized her talent from the beginning, he'd had some doubts about how much he'd enjoy being a mentor.

Perhaps if the girl had turned out to be a fool, I would have regretted it, but there is great pleasure to be found in spending time improving another person.

CHAPTER SEVENTEEN

Myna tilted her head as she studied an orange and brown terracotta Mycenean jar. An octopus and fish were painted on the sides. Alison watched her and curiosity bubbled in her head.

She's looked so interested since we entered the museum but she's barely said anything. Maybe I should have taken her to Kizuki to get some ramen instead. The woman loves her Earth noodles.

The old Drow moved closer to the glass that separated her from the jar. Her cool gaze flicked to the side as she read the description of the vase. "For such a short-lived species, humans have a good respect for their past."

A few people eyed the woman after the comment. Her night-black skin in combination with her bright white hair and pointed ears made her noticeable even in a place as diverse as Seattle. The high-necked dress and huge skirt made her stand out even more.

Other visitors had taken surreptitious pictures of the

two of them, but Alison wasn't sure who they were interested in.

Alison tilted her head as she looked at the vase. "History can seem more important when you've not lived through it. Now that we know a lot of our history on Earth isn't what we thought, it's even more interesting." She chuckled. "But my mother is a history and archaeology professor, so I'm basically required to say something like that."

Myna looked away from the jar and walked to another display case that contained two ceramic figurines of women holding snakes. "You told me you would be leaving on a job soon."

"Yes, tomorrow. I'm not sure how long I'll be gone, but probably at least a week. Why?"

"I would think you have more important things to do than spend the day before such an important task showing me Earth culture."

Alison moved over to inspect the plaque that described the figurines.

SNAKE GODDESS FIGURINES
NEO-PALATIAL MYCENEAN, 1750-1450 BC
So-called Snake Goddess figurines were first discovered by British archaeologist Arthur Evans who located two such figurines and declared one a "Snake Goddess" and another a "Snake Priestess." Although most have been found in house sanctuaries in Mycenean ruins and were previously associated with household goddess traditions, new cross-cultural comparison data based on modern post-gate revised archaeology theories suggests they might, in fact, be meant to symbolize powerful

local witches who extended their protection to the local community.

In other cultures, the irregular visits of Earth-born magic users and Oricerans from hidden kemanas has been associated with legends of mythical beings, but research and study remain ongoing in the Mycenean context.

"Protection, huh?" she murmured. "The gates weren't open then, but they were still doing their best."

Myna narrowed her eyes. "Just because I'm not as familiar with all the social standards of human culture doesn't mean I can't see through such feeble attempts, my princess. Do not mistake me being a Drow for being a fool. I know what 'dodging the question' is."

Alison grimaced. "That's not what I tried to do." She shook her head and gestured at the various artifacts on stands and glass displays cases. "This is supposed to be a thank you, not an insult."

"A thank you?" Her companion looked confused.

"I don't do enough to thank you, and I'm not even talking about your...sacrifice." She stared down at one of the small cracked figurines, perhaps the last record of someone like her from thousands of years before. "I run a security company, and when I'm not on jobs, I'm worrying about dark wizards. My life is centered around violence and I've done nothing but bring you into that, even if indirectly."

Myna frowned. "Peace has its place, but it must be maintained by strength. The Drow are warriors."

Alison raised a hand to quiet the other woman. "I know. I'm not saying I plan to suddenly become a pacifist. The kind of people I've eliminated are the worst kind of scum. The fact that almost every country has bounty hunters to deal with out-of-control magical threats is proof enough that we can't simply talk our way out of problems."

The old Drow nodded and a satisfied look settled over her face. "Then why did you mention that your life is centered around violence?"

"I thought about when you told me about your arrival on Earth. How you fought with Triads."

"What about that?"

"That was the first place you arrived, but it wasn't like you immediately came to me after that."

Myna shook her head. "I visited several places. After Hong Kong, I sought lands of conflict where the strong trampled the weak. I searched for a champion. I searched for you."

Alison frowned. "That's what I was worried about."

"I thought you no longer had a problem with my service to you as a Drow princess." A hint of offense colored the woman's tone. She lifted her chin and squared her shoulders.

"That's not what I'm saying," Alison replied. She paused to search for the right words. "It's more about your impression of Earth. It must seem tremendously violent to you, much more so than Oriceran."

"It's more unstable than Oriceran in some ways, but it's not like Oriceran lacks for violence and petty beings who would kill for no other reason than to satisfy their own avarice. This planet had at least a single dominant intelligent race, and you could reach for your commonalities more than many races on Oriceran have been able to. That is why our greatest war was more frightening than yours."

Myna relayed the words with cool detachment as she walked over to an intricately-patterned replica Mycenean rug. "I don't look down on Earth if that's your concern. It took this planet another ten thousand years compared to Oriceran to reach the point of being able to destroy itself, and that limits calls to Oriceran superiority. What good are power and knowledge if you burn and wreck lands with it? Blaming Rhazdon for it all is easy but short-sighted. A truly peaceful world wouldn't have been dragged into war."

Alison folded her arms and nodded at the rug. "The point is that I wanted to thank you by spending time with you that didn't require the use of magic. I don't want you to always have to be in pain around me. The non-violent part of Earth offers more than tasty noodle carts, so I thought this would be a good place to go."

"I see. I have seen more of the lands of Earth if that's your concern, my princess."

She smiled. "It is, but if I can do my small part today to help you have a positive experience on Earth, then that'll go a small way toward paying you back for all your help with my magic, let alone your sacrifice."

Myna turned toward her with a soft smile. "I appreciate your gesture. Perhaps this will help me to understand better why you don't wish to become queen."

Alison laughed. "As I told someone not all that long ago who asked if I was interested in politics, I'd be spectacularly bad at it."

The Drow's face became a mask of pure incredulity.

"Are you so sure? You're strong and honorable. What more do you truly need?"

"I don't know. Maybe some sort of actual deep and thorough understanding of the needs of the Drow people?" She shrugged. "At least in the American system, the other branches can keep the president from fucking up too badly. I know things are temporarily different with the Drow, but if I became queen, I could lead them down a messed-up path exactly like Laena."

"Or a new path of glory and improvement," her companion countered.

"It took an outsider—my dad—to get rid of the last bad queen," Alison scoffed. "Unless you have another one of him lying around, that suggests the Drow should be careful before they put anyone in charge who doesn't know what they're doing." She sighed. "I don't think I can ever be what you want or need me to be. My Drow heritage has gifted me with magic, but I was raised a human and I still think like a human."

Myna released a low, throaty chuckle. "For now. Pure humans die so early. Will you still think like a human when you're two centuries old? Three?"

A young woman frowned at the old Drow in passing. The new arrival pulled her purse tighter against her and hurried on without looking back.

Alison ignored the rude woman as she considered the implications of what her companion had told her. "We don't know that I'll live as long as a normal Drow."

"Yes, we do." She moved from the rug to several polished swords and a gold necklace in another display case. "You forget how much I've examined you. I don't understand what Earth science might say about you, but to my magic, you feel like a full Drow. I'm confident you will live six to eight centuries like most Drow."

Alison walked over to the display case and leaned forward to examine the necklace in more detail. She'd thought it was a series of simple shapes before, but on closer inspection, she made out the eagle design of each individual link in the necklace. "So you think that in a couple of hundred years, I'll come to my senses and become Queen of the Drow?"

"No, that'd take too long," Myna responded. "Especially with some of the other princesses interested in becoming queen. For all the patience that comes with being long-lived, rulership transitions among our people are typically swift. It surprises me that they've waited this long to choose a new queen."

"Maybe they'll go American-style and give up on royalty."

The old woman scoffed. "That is doubtful."

"And what if you're wrong? What if I never become Queen of the Drow?"

"Then nothing. You forget, my princess, why I sought you out—not only because you were a princess but also because of how you used the legacy of the Shadow Forged." Myna walked over to her and placed a hand on her shoulder. "You embody true Drow honor and strength. If my instincts are wrong and you never ascend the throne, then so be it. I've still aided a powerful warrior who will wield her strength to make her country and planet a better place." She lowered her hand. "And it pleases me that you wanted to show me this place."

The Drow spun on her boot heel and hurried toward the other end of the exhibit. "Let's not waste your thoughtfulness, my princess. We still have much of this floor to see. Let's give your Earth even more chance to impress me."

Alison smiled and headed after her.

I can't give her much that she cares about, but I can at least give her this.

CHAPTER EIGHTEEN

Mason shook the sleeping Alison and her eyes fluttered open.

"I'm awake," she mumbled. It took her a few seconds to remember she was on a small private jet owned by Abigail Wilson. The CEO sat a few seats ahead of her and worked through some notes on a tablet.

They'd flown on a chartered supersonic flight to Lisbon and boarded another smaller subsonic plane to the island.

Abigail turned and smiled at her. The woman had a couple of decades on her and lacked the smooth skin of youth, but she retained a natural elegance and beauty. A few white streaks had infiltrated her hair, but it was nothing compared to Alison's white mane.

It's age for her and not Drow blood, but she also doesn't worry about dyeing it. I can respect that.

"I'm glad you're awake," Abigail said quietly. "I think that even you'll be impressed, Miss Brownstone." She nodded toward the window. "This is the outer layer of the defenses for Nereid Island I told you about."

A huge wall of dark clouds filled the horizon. Bolts of lightning blazed through them at regular intervals.

Hana stared out the window, wide-eyed, and Mason looked a little awed.

Drysi, who sat in the row behind Alison, yawned as she also woke and noticed the storm. "Bloody hell. I know you said they'll make a hole in that for us, but your pilot is a brave bastard to fly toward something like that on purpose."

Abigail chuckled with real amusement. "We'll turn toward the island soon. It's taken slightly longer to establish radio contact with the Nereids than we anticipated, but they're now making preparations to lower the defenses."

Alison tilted her head, mesmerized by the patterns in the clouds and lightning. In absolute terms, the island and storm were tiny, barely worthy of notice for most of the world, but the level of magical energy on display was staggering.

Is this what everywhere on Earth will be like in a few centuries?

"I'm starting to understand why people want the aventurine," she conceded.

Abigail nodded and turned her green eyes back toward the storm. "The Nereids allow only a very small amount to be harvested overall, but for the needs of technomagic companies, it's more than sufficient."

Drysi continued to stare out the window, concern on her face. "Alison explained the details of the job and the Nereids to me, but I don't understand why no one else has already mined the stuff. This can't be the first time they've reached out."

"No," the CEO responded with a light shake of her head. "They've gone through several companies in the last ten years, which was when they first reached out. The immediate predecessor had their contract terminated when the Nereids learned that they had harvested more material than permitted and risked the release of certain dangerous forms of contamination from the mining areas."

Alison frowned and spun toward her. "Contamination?"

"From what I understand, a type of magical pollution. The Nereids are rather determined to remain on this island. Their kind has continuously inhabited it since the last time the gates were open. One of the reasons they're willing to meet with me is that I eagerly agreed to their strict supervision rules, and I'm willing to allow them to use a truth detection spell on me."

The Welsh witch winced. "That's invasive."

"Yes, but I understand where they're coming from and I also can understand that they wouldn't want to be forced to leave their ancient home because of an industrial accident. But don't worry. We won't go near any contamination zones."

Drysi mumbled something under her breath.

Mason frowned. "From what you told me, Abigail, no one but Nereids live on the island. So how does the extraction work? Is it all automatic?"

Abigail's laugh had a merry quality to it. "No. There isn't sufficient power infrastructure for that. It's all rather inconvenient. Aeternum will probably do what the last company did, which was maintain a ship with a helipad outside the island and fly the workers in during the morning and back out at night, then cycle them to and from Portugal."

"I'm surprised this island isn't in the Mediterranean," Alison commented.

He looked quickly at her. "Why's that, A?"

"Oh, I thought about that because of that museum trip I took with Myna. There was so much Mycenaean and ancient Greek stuff there. These Nereids inspired Greek myth, but they're farther to the west."

"Yeah, but that was a long time ago. They might have lived in the Mediterranean when the gates were still open."

"Good point," she agreed.

"You have to be kidding me!" Hana shouted. She bounced in her seat. "Look at the storm."

Mason nodded in appreciation. "That is damned impressive."

The storm parted as if a huge, invisible Titan had cleaved through it with a blade. The clouds and lightning banked on either side to allow a clear flight path toward the tiny, mountainous, forested island.

The plane banked toward the new opening.

"It's much more impressive than a Mountain Strider," Alison admitted.

"Miss Wilson," the pilot's gruff voice said over the intercom. "We've received clearance to land, and as I'm sure you can see, they've opened the door. I'd like everyone in their seats in case things get bumpy. Welcome to Nereid Island."

The aircraft lined up with the exposed island and began its descent.

Drysi gripped her armrests so hard her fingers turned white.

"Don't you like flying?" Alison asked.

"I don't like flying into something like that." She managed a weak nod toward the storm. "If those Nereids decided at the last second that they wanted to end us, there's nothing we could do about it."

Abigail smiled. "I've worked to set this meeting up for months. I'm confident that they harbor no ill intent."

"I get that," the witch replied. She took a deep breath and released her death grip on the seats. "And that you're risking your life here, so at least you have skin in the game. But I won't lie, I think I'd rather raid a warehouse full of bounties than fly through a thin doorway in a magical storm."

The plane descended farther. More of the details of their destination came into view, including a single long, dark airstrip near the edge of the island and a long stretch of rocky beach.

"I don't see any radar or anything like that," Alison commented.

"It's not like they have to worry about air traffic control," Hana replied. "Or even invasions with that kind of protection surrounding the island."

Abigail nodded. "There is almost no technology on the island except for whatever is brought in for the extraction operations, and it all has to be battery or solar powered for the Nereids to tolerate its presence. Even the radio communication is done via magic." She tapped at the window. "See those small dark dots clustered away from the airstrip but still along the beach area?"

Alison tilted her head and narrowed her eyes. She nodded when she finally spotted them.

"That's where all the Nereids live," Abigail continued. "There are only fifty of them, so they don't need much space. From my understanding, they mostly rely on seaweed as their primary food source."

The plane continued its descent and the airstrip grew larger with each passing second.

"A handful of Oricerans living on this island with almost no contact with the outside world after the gates closed for thousands of years," Alison murmured. "That's unusual even by Oriceran standards. Hiding in a kemana or something is one thing, but a place like this?"

Hana frowned. "Why can't they go back to Oriceran again?"

"My understanding is that it has to do with the nature of the seawater on Earth and its interaction with magic," Abigail explained. "They've become too attuned to it to survive a return to Oriceran."

Mason chuckled. "I think I'd get bored. It's like living with your extended family, except in this case, your relatives live centuries and there's not even a new cousin until one of them dies."

Hana's hand remained on the window, her eyes still wide as before and an almost childlike excitement on her face. "Too bad Sonya and Tahir didn't come."

Alison smiled. "I think Tahir would spend most of the time complaining, but at least this way, he has some extra time to train Sonya and get her started on her league."

"True."

They fell silent as the plane finished its descent and

finally touched down with a slight bump. The lift spoilers were all raised and the force of the deceleration pressed the passengers against their seatbelts. The jet's speed dropped rapidly until it eventually came to a stop.

"Ladies and our single gentleman," the pilot announced, "welcome to Nereid Island."

Alison took a step off the airstairs. Now that she was on the ground, the jagged mountains that hadn't looked that impressive compared to the Cascades from the air loomed over her, oppressive in their own way. The forests were thick enough to hide an entire army. Oaks, cypress, and pine dominated. Despite the massive dark clouds surrounding the island, the sun shone brightly in the sky.

Could someone sneak in if they went high enough?

Two Nereids stood ten yards away. The tall, lithe, hair-less sea-green women both had pointed ears and solid dark-blue eyes. Blue and green striations of various shades infused their skin. A light layer of moisture covered them as if they'd just left the ocean. They were barefoot, exposing their webbed toes, and all wore the same simple shifts made of twisted seaweed. Alison couldn't help but think of it as Poseidon's macramé.

Abigail stepped forward. She placed her palms together and bowed, a traditional Nereid greeting from what she'd told Alison. "I'm Abigail Wilson. On behalf of Aeternum and myself, let me express how honored I am that you have agreed to meet with me." She gestured to the Brownstone contractors. "This is my security detail. As per our earlier agreement, all are magicals."

One of the Nereids stepped forward. It was difficult for Alison to tell them apart, but there were subtle differences in the patterns on their skin when she examined them closer.

"I am Der," the woman announced, and her voice had an odd resonant and melodic quality. She placed her palms together and bowed her head to Abigail. "Welcome to our island. We hope this exchange will prove fruitful. We recognize that not all humans are as duplicitous as the ones we've dealt with in the past."

"Again, thank you for the opportunity." The CEO kept a polite smile on her face.

She has excellent self-control. We both lead companies, but we're very different women and leaders.

The other Nereid moved forward and tilted her head as she stared at the plane. "It's so fascinating, your plane. I never find these uninteresting. These and helicopters."

"Do not touch the outsider's machine, Ine," Der commanded. "You might damage it."

Ine turned toward Abigail. "I applaud your bravery. As interesting as they are, I wouldn't want to rely on something so unreliable as technology. I've spoken with other humans about crashes."

Alison smiled. A different perspective was always interesting. She trusted in her magic, but she'd always viewed magic as far more capricious than the products of Earth's science and engineering.

The CEO smiled in response. "This is practically magic

compared to the kind of things humans used to fly in. It doesn't take much bravery, especially with a good pilot."

The pilot, Kenneth, remained on the plane. From what Abigail explained, the Nereids were uncomfortable with more than one male on the island given what had happened with the previous company, as unfair as the generalization was. They only allowed Mason to accompany Abigail because the CEO had been rather insistent.

She trusts him with her life. He spent years as a bodyguard. How many people out there did he save?

"You must excuse Ine," Der explained, her face tight. "She's fascinated by the outside world. She's so eager and volunteered to help with this, so I couldn't resist allowing her some reward."

The Nereid looked slowly at each of the new arrivals, suspicion on her face in contrast to Ine's broad smile.

Der's attention shifted to Mason and lingered for a moment before she turned to Hana. Some of the suspicion vanished when she looked at the girl, but her nostrils flared as she turned toward Alison. "You look human, but you're not. You're a Drow, aren't you? I've never met one, but you feel like how they've been described to me."

"And how is that exactly?"

"It's hard to explain—like a smoldering fire in a chilly room. Like shadows touching the soul."

Alison nodded slowly and her smile faded. "Half-Drow. My biological father was a human and my mother was a full-blooded Drow."

Walt didn't even deserve the dignity of being called her father, but Alison didn't want to interject any unnecessary tension into the negotiations by bringing up too much of her complicated family history.

"Interesting," Der replied. "The Drow must have changed far more than I've realized."

She shrugged. "I'm the only one I know of, but I can't be certain."

Ine scoffed. "Of course the Drow have changed. The humans have changed. Everyone's changed. It's been thousands of years. Change is inevitable. Time is like the tide. It'll wear you down."

Der gave her a look of warning and the other Nereid pursed her lips and stepped back with a slight frown.

Abigail cleared her throat. "Perhaps this is a good time to show us to our accommodations?"

The Nereid leader turned toward the village in the distance without further comment. A thin layer of smooth soil surrounded the airstrip on the water side before it gave way to rocky beach. The village, such as it was, was a collection of small, dark wooden buildings that lined the edge of the sand. Most looked like they might house one occupant or maybe two. A single large, circular building stood in the center.

The construction itself lacked the angular precision typical of human buildings. The island tree source of the wood remained obvious, but magic had been used to twist and weave the wood together to produce buildings that looked more like something that had grown out of the ground than products of purposeful construction. None of the structures had doors.

A few Nereids wandered the beach and gathered seaweed in a small basket. Others collected driftwood. A few frolicked nude in the water. All glanced toward the outsiders as they approached the village.

Alison glanced at Mason, but he barely paid the naked green women any attention. Instead, his gaze swept the village, his eyes full of speculation.

He's doing what he's good at, looking for threats. He won't let his guard down.

Der gestured to a small cluster of three huts as everyone moved closer. "You'll stay in these. In a few hours, we shall have a feast in your honor."

Hana smiled sheepishly. "Um, what exactly will the menu be?"

Alison managed to restrain her laughter. It was a good question. As an amateur chef, she wasn't sure how much she trusted a group of women who relied on nothing but seaweed. Sure, she loved the salty nutty crunch of good nori, but that wasn't a whole meal.

Ine smiled. "I'll handle food preparation. Your meals during your time here will consist of roasted fresh fish along with berries and fruits gathered from the forest. We have these in abundance here even if we don't eat them ourselves."

"Oh," the fox replied and didn't bother to hide her surprise. "That actually sounds good." She winced. "Sorry, no offense intended."

Ine laughed. "You're interesting."

"I try to be."

Der nodded to Abigail. "We shall begin negotiations tomorrow."

"That's fine with me," the CEO responded.

Alison smiled as gentle waves crashed on the shore. The

powerful storm surrounding the island didn't seem to affect anything on the inside. It might be unsettling, but with the sun still overhead, she could see how the Nereids had grown comfortable in their hidden and protected paradise.

This will be the easiest job I've had in a while.

CHAPTER NINETEEN

A couple of hours later, Alison's team knelt at the central table inside the circular building that served as the village meeting hall. The interior of the hall resembled the huts in that it was simple and utilitarian. A few carved driftwood figurines of Nereids, fish, sharks, and whales hung on the walls, but there was no other decoration. Summoned orbs circled the ceiling to provide light.

Most of the Nereids in the village had gathered for the feast and a handful attended to some evening duties. Alison tried not to be amused by so many Nereids munching on fresh seaweed from trays, but every once in a while, she had to look down and cover her mouth.

When she had heard about the seaweed earlier, she'd imagined something like the Japanese nori used in sushi —something that was compressed and dried—but the seaweed eaten by their hosts looked like it'd been harvested directly from the ocean or beach and much of it was still wet. She even recognized some of the strands from the earlier beach harvest.

The guests and hosts had exchanged light conversation, mostly about the state of the outside world. Many of the Nereids seemed curious about the most banal of events, particularly Ine, and it was obvious they had almost no access to regular news.

Is that better or worse than being saturated with it like we are? Not hearing about the billionaires on trial wouldn't have hurt me much, but if I'd not known about the Friends of Carlyle, we might not have put together the plan that removed them before they caused trouble.

Is ignorance bliss? It's been a long time since I haven't had to worry about every small piece of darkness out there.

Alison plopped a tangy berry into her mouth and munched. Magically deboned fillets of roasted fish rested on wooden trays, and she'd already eaten several. The Nereids hadn't provided any utensils, but the preparation of the fish didn't necessitate any. Water was provided in wooden cups and their hosts refilled them with magic, but there was no alcohol. Maybe it wasn't paradise after all.

"I apologize if my sisters annoy you with their persistent questions," Der ventured after Abigail fielded three questions in a row. "We get so little news from the outside world. The storm makes it difficult to speak other than at close distances. I don't see how it affects us, so I don't care, but they find it intriguing. And it's been some months since we last had outsiders."

"I'm not offended or annoyed," the CEO replied. "I'm more than happy to do what it takes to establish a positive relationship with your island."

Alison swallowed her berry and enjoyed the residual aftertaste. "I'm curious. Why are you so thorough with the defenses to the point that even radio signals have difficulty? I can understand that back when magic was secret, this level of protection might have been necessary, but it doesn't seem like you need it anymore. Aventurine has its uses, but this isn't 1255. You won't be invaded by random Viking raiders looking for your minerals."

Ine nodded. "That is true. It's something I've said for some time."

She withered under a harsh look from Der.

Huh. I guess I touched a nerve. Maybe that was a stupid thing to ask. I barely have my own life figured out, so who I am to suggest that they don't know what they're doing?

On the other hand, Ine seems to agree. Maybe that doesn't make a full point for me, but a half point, at least.

"Pirates or raiders, no," Der responded, her harsh gaze still fixed on the other Nerein. "Armies, yes. Considering that human nations still war with each other over resources, it'd be foolish—given how few of us are here—to not make sure we can protect ourselves without relying on outsiders. Even with the magical energy available to us here, without the storm, a few bombs or powerful attack spells could kill us all. We've experienced enough recent human greed not to rely too much on humanity's forbearance when considering our future. As our ancestors left Oriceran during the war, we don't trust them to defend us either."

"The Great War's been over a long time," Alison pointed out.

"It doesn't matter. The potential's always there."

She decided not to press farther. When she glanced at

Abigail, the other woman didn't seem annoyed. She simply sipped her water and watched in silence.

I'm only the security. Maybe I should keep my mouth shut. On the other hand, Abigail might be happy that she doesn't have to talk for a few minutes.

Mason nodded. "Why live here, though? On this specific island? I know you need the magical energy, but why not in a kemana? You'd probably be safer if you had more magicals around, and you'd have more chance to interact with the rest of the world."

Der shook her head. "We've been here for thousands of years. It's our home. We have a fundamental connection to the place that we wouldn't have living in a kemana elsewhere. As our sisters die, a new one is born from the sea, but only from the ocean we have a true connection to. For us to leave this place now would be for our sisterhood to die. There are other Nereids on Oriceran, but our sisterhood is our own. We might live longer than humans, but we're also not gnomes. If we leave this place, the direct memory of it will fade within mere centuries."

"That's understandable to me even as a human," Abigail concurred. "Family is important."

"Part of survival is adapting to the world you're in," Ine suggested.

"We've survived." Der narrowed her eyes. "Not only that, we've persevered for thousands of years. There's no reason to change our way of life. The gates being open is of no real relevance other than the fact that it allows trade for more resources."

If you really didn't care, you wouldn't set up a mining deal, though. You're still trying to plan for the future in the back of your mind, aren't you, Der?

Hana gobbled several more bites of fish. "I'm sorry to interrupt, but I need to say again how delicious this is. If you ever want to make this place a resort, you can make Ine the chef. Nereid by the Sea and all that."

Ine smiled but it didn't reach her eyes. "That would be lovely. That's another way to reach out to the world. Let them come to you instead of going to them. Open the gates rather than locking them so only friends can enter."

Der scoffed. "Enemies can also walk through open gates."

An awkward silence settled over the table. Even Abigail seemed at a loss as to what to say. Alison, for her part, had no idea how to comment on the family relations of an isolated population of Oriceran sea nymphs. She was there to make sure no one hurt the CEO and nothing else.

There aren't even any dark wizards involved in this. It's not my business.

Drysi took a sip of her water and cleared her throat. "This might be rude, but I'm curious about the storm. It's not a normal spell or ritual, is it? If it were, I think the magic would feel overwhelming, but I barely can sense it over the normal magic around here. That's right strange considering how powerful it is."

"We use an artifact," Ine admitted. "It'd be weak else-where, but with magic reserves from the aventurine on this island, it can protect us. The aventurine also fuels the wards and the other spells we need to keep ourselves...locked in."

Der glared at the other Nereid. "You go too far, Ine."

Ine ignored her. "If you trust Aeternum to mine here, they would learn this anyway. I don't like all this dissembling. It's too much like humans."

"Enough," the leader snapped. "Remove yourself from us. We have our reasons for our way of living as you know all too well, including our *duty*."

Duty? Damn, laying down family duty is a stiletto to the heart move there. Talk about some major sister-on-sister emotional violence.

All conversation in the rest of the room ceased and all the Nereids stared at the center table.

Ine stood, her smile still on her face. "You cannot fight the tide, sister. It will wear even you down." She stood, placed her palms together, and bowed before she headed toward the small open doorway that led out of the central structure.

Der closed her eyes and inhaled deeply. "I apologize. We don't usually air our disagreements in front of outsiders. Things have been chaotic since we terminated the last contract."

Abigail pursed her lips as she watched the other woman leave the building. "Is she young for your kind?"

"I lead because I was chosen by my sisters, not because of age." The Nereid shook her head. "She's older than I am and believes we should open ourselves more to the world. Perhaps we will once we can stabilize the aventurine situation, but there are things Ine chooses to ignore about this place."

"I understand," the CEO responded. "I hope I can be a part of establishing a positive relationship between your island and the rest of the world."

"We shall see."

Alison concentrated on the berries and recognized that no matter what the species, family trouble revolved around the same kinds of issues.

A sharp scream from outside was immediately followed by a pulse of magic.

The half-Drow scrambled to her feet and rushed toward the exit. She pointed at Abigail. "Mason, Hana, stay with Abigail. Drysi, with me." She summoned a quick shield as she sprinted toward the exit.

The bounty hunter drew an enchanted throwing knife before she even found her feet.

The two women barreled out of the building. The bright moon reflected off the water and allowed clear visibility up and down the beach without any need for magic.

It didn't matter. There were no enemies anywhere but there was trouble, though.

Ine lay on the ground a few feet away, curled up as she clutched her abdomen. Thick blue blood leaked from a deep, jagged slash.

Alison extended a shadow blade and rushed to her side, spun, and looked for her attacker. "Who did this to you?"

Drysi stood back and drew her gun to join her knife.

"A...a shadow," Ine managed through clenched teeth. She raised a shaky arm to point in the distance toward the plane. "It came from that way and he went that way."

"He? What did he look like?"

The Nereid shrugged weakly. "It could be a woman. I don't know for sure. Humanoid."

Der and several other Nereids stepped out of the building.

"She needs healing," Alison called. "She was attacked."

Der rushed to Ine and knelt in front of her. She placed her hands on the wounded abdomen. Water seeped from her palms and covered the wound. The laceration began to seal itself a few seconds later.

Abigail walked out of the meeting hall with a concerned look. Hana and Mason stood on either side of her, both with their guns drawn. The red glow of the crystal ring confirmed that Hana's defenses were up. Her claws were extended, and her tails stood rigid behind her. Alison assumed Mason had a shield spell up, but it was hard to tell with all the background magical energy of the island itself.

Ine sat up, her wound now healed. "He...it was like a shadow. It moved past me and hurt me before it moved toward the plane."

"I didn't see anything," Alison replied. "So they might have invisibility magic. Damn it."

Der frowned. "What have you brought here?"

"Us?" Alison asked. "We didn't bring anything."

"An enemy has come with your plane. Our sister was attacked."

Drysi snorted. "They might have sneaked in when you let the storm down. Keeping your eye out for the bloody bastards is as important as keeping your door locked."

Abigail sighed. "The most important thing now is to find the assailant before someone else is hurt."

"I agree," Alison replied crisply. Shadow wings sprouted from her back. "I'll do some aerial recon, but it might be best to gather all the Nereids at the meeting hall."

Der frowned. "We can defend ourselves."

She pointed to Ine. "Are you sure of that?"

The Nereid stood, fear etched on her face. "They're offering to help us, sister."

"They should," Der spat. "It's their fault this evil is on us —and that's assuming they didn't purposefully bring a killer."

I hate to think it, but she might be right. But I don't get it. We checked everything, including the luggage on both planes. No one was on board.

"Now wait one dam—" Mason began.

Abigail stopped him with the shake of the head. "I'm willing to submit myself to a truth spell right now if that's what it takes to get you to believe me."

The life wizard muttered under his breath. "Me, too."

Drysi waved, the knife still in hand. "If that's what's trending right now, I'm in."

"I have nothing to hide," Hana replied.

Alison rolled her eyes. "I'll do what it takes as long as it's quick. The longer it takes, the more chance we risk that the attacker will escape."

Der's gaze cut from Abigail to Ine. "How do we know he's not hiding in your plane, simply waiting until it's time for you to leave?"

"We can check the plane together," she suggested reasonably. "Now, let's—"

The plane exploded and illuminated the runway with a scorching orange-red ball of flame. Metal shrapnel rained from the sky. The destruction was accompanied by a pulse of magic.

Alison scrubbed a hand down her face. "Or not."

CHAPTER TWENTY

Abigail gasped and turned toward the plane. "Kenneth!"

Mason grabbed her arm. "Don't. It's not safe."

"But Kenneth was in there," she shouted, her face pale. "He's not a magical, and he doesn't have any artifacts. We have to save him."

"It's too late." The wizard shook his head and his grim expression made no effort to hide the truth or spare her feelings. "I'm sorry, Abigail. There's nothing anyone can do for him now."

Alison gritted her teeth. *How the hell did this job go crazy in only a few minutes? We're supposed to be eating fish, not losing people to explosions.*

Stone-faced, Der frowned at the burning plane wreckage in the distance. She leaned across to whisper to another Nereid and fear lingered in her solid blue eyes. The other nymph rushed back into the meeting hall.

"I'll check it out," Alison announced. "Everyone else, stay here." She elevated and flew toward the runway where she circled the flaming debris. There was no shadow man or any suspicious movements. Kenneth's charred corpse lay farther up the runway, the remains of his pilot's uniform still identifiable.

I'm sorry, Kenneth. We'll find whoever did this to you. I promise.

The low notes of a blown conch cut through the night. The Nereid had emerged from the meeting hall with a shell. She blew again and the volume grew far louder than would be possible without the aid of magic.

Alison expanded her search radius and stopped when she noticed something small and glowing that floated a few feet off the ground on the other side of the runway. She'd missed it before in all the flames. Once she'd layered a few more shields around herself, she flew toward the object and hovered cautiously a few yards away.

What the hell is this thing?

The conch sounded again.

She wasn't sure what the glowing object was, but it resembled a lotus seed pod. With a puff, it spat out sparkling particles that drifted high into the air.

Is this what blew the plane up?

After a moment, she frowned and flew back to the gathered Nereids and her team. She landed lightly, more confused than before she had examined the wreckage.

"Kenneth?" Abigail asked, her voice weak.

Alison shook her head. "I'm sorry. He's already dead."

The CEO swallowed and nodded. She took a few deep breaths before she squared her shoulders. "But you'll make his killer pay, though, right? I don't believe an exploding plane is an accident, not right after the attack on Ine."

I have to give it to her. She's a tough woman for someone not involved in something like security.

"No other innocent needs to die on this island," Alison responded, her voice low and full of dangerous promise.

Were we sloppy? Should we have left someone to guard the plane?

She turned to Der. There were a few things she needed to figure out before they could come up with a plan of action. "What's up with the shell?"

"We were gathering the last of our sisters for safety as suggested," Der replied, her forehead creased with real concern. "I apologize for my earlier outburst. I'm simply worried. Such...violence is rare in our sanctuary."

"We'll stop whoever attacked Ine and the plane," Alison insisted. "You have my word on that. Are all your people accounted for?"

Der shook her head. "One of our sisters didn't answer the call."

"Are you sure she's not too far away and didn't hear it?"

"Yes. The few who were not at the meal would have been outside and nearby. None of us travels far from the village at night." The nymph's voice quivered at the end.

What is she hiding?

Alison pointed at the plane. "Were they doing something with weird glowing seedpods? I saw one near the wreckage."

Der's breath caught. Several of the Nereids stared at Alison. Others looked away, even more fear in their eyes.

"No," the leader replied, her voice unnaturally even and flat. "I think it's best that you destroy that immediately. It wasn't responsible for the plane or attacking Ine, but it represents a clear danger."

"Huh?"

"It's obviously dangerous, wouldn't you say?" She blinked several times. "It needs to be destroyed. We can't deal with multiple troubles right now."

Alison frowned. "What is it? What is going on here? I don't know what that thing is, but I guarantee you we didn't bring it with us, which means it was already here. And you seem to know what it is."

She stared out at the sea. "We don't have time to discuss such things at the moment. We need to find our sister. You should return to the pod and destroy it while the rest of us search."

"I need you to tell me what the hell it is before I do anything." Alison gestured to Abigail. "She lost one of her people. It wasn't that long ago that you blamed us, but I found something odd and now, you're acting weird and cagey."

"Are you implying we were responsible for the attacks?" Der's nostrils flared.

"Alison, please," Abigail cautioned. "We're all on edge, but we shouldn't insult our hosts."

Always the businesswoman to the end, huh? Well, I'm in a different kind of business, and it's not one you do by being nice and worrying about people's feelings.

Hana tilted her head as she stared into the distance. "Alison, I hate to call you out, but I think you were wrong."

She glanced quickly at her friend. "What do you mean?"

"I think Kenneth's alive." The fox pointed toward the

plane. A shadowy form cloaked in fire sprinted toward the gathering.

"He is?" Abigail's eyes widened. "Can't you use magic to heal him?"

"If he's still alive, sure, but, there's no damned way he survived that explosion." Alison frowned. She didn't feel the need to describe the awful state of the body to Abigail, so she'd make her certainty clear in a different way. She extended a shadow blade. "I don't think it's Kenneth. I think it's whoever sliced Ine open and blew the plane up."

Mason stepped forward and aimed his gun.

Hana raised hers. "I'm glad we didn't bring Sonya along."

Drysi sighed. "I'm beginning to think, Alison, that your claim that this would be an easy job was a teeny bit off." She readied her throwing knife. "Not tidy at all."

Alison snorted. "Yeah, I won't argue with you there."

"You must destroy the pod first!" Der shouted. "It's more important than whatever enemy is approaching us."

Another humanoid form rose from the ground to join the charging man.

Several of the Nereids cried out in fear. "It's too late."

"It's not too late, sisters," Der insisted. "We will use the countermagic to protect everyone, then we will use the ritual."

Alison narrowed her eyes. "We will have another conversation very soon, and it'll be a lot more detailed than the one we just had."

The two assailants closed but slowed as they grew closer.

Hana was right. One of those who approached had

most likely been Kenneth judging by the cracked and charred skin and the remains of the uniform. Now, however, his eyes glowed soft yellow and green frond-like growths had sprouted over much of the body. Sharp dark-green barbs extended from his fingers. A complex web of roots extended into his head and led to a small dark-green lotus-like flower that grew over his heart.

The other new arrival was easily recognizable as a Nereid. Her plant-covered body hadn't been damaged as badly as Kenneth's had, but a similar parasitic flower lay embedded in her chest and its roots extended into her head.

Fuck. Am I looking at what I think I am? Motherfucking plant zombies.

The two creatures advanced slowly.

"Are they suddenly afraid?" Alison asked.

Abigail stared in horror at the remains of her pilot. "He deserved better than this. Far better than this."

A Nereid screamed and tried to run.

Der grabbed her arm and yanked her back. "Stay together. Let the outsiders face them. If we run without taking appropriate measures, we'll lose more than one sister tonight. We must remain calm when dealing with them."

She released the other nymph who remained unhappily in place.

"The original bodies are already dead," Ine explained. Her gaze was fixed on the advancing zombies and her normally melodious voice was hollow and distant. "We can't save the others. Don't let them touch you or you risk becoming tainted."

Alison layered another shield over herself. "My team all use shields."

"With enough attacks, they can penetrate such things."

Alison snorted. "Of course. Anti-magic plant zombies."

The two monsters twitched and jerked their heads back and forth.

"Why don't they attack?" Drysi asked and her gaze darted from one to the other. "Don't they want to eat our fucking brains or some shit?"

"It's not like that," Ine replied quietly. "The Curse Flower that controls their bodies has some small access to what they once were, including their memories. They're probably trying to determine who to kill first to weaken us. That's what they do. It's part of the magic that made them."

"What the hell?" Alison barked.

Der flung an arm toward the meeting hall entrance. "Sisters, get inside there. Everyone, protect one another."

"You should get in there, too, Abigail," Alison recommended. "This will get messy."

The zombies' heads continued to jerk as they evaluated the possible targets.

Ine stood transfixed, a mixture of horror and curiosity on her face. Der grabbed her by the hand and yanked her toward the meeting hall. Abigail blinked several times before she registered what she'd been told to do and turned to leave.

The two zombies surged directly toward the CEO. She backpedaled and tripped.

Mason threw himself in front of her and opened fire, and Hana joined him. The zombies lurched at the impacts but continued their attack. Alison rushed toward them and swung her shadow blade to decapitate both in one clean strike.

They didn't fall and the now headless bodies twitched and clawed at her. Their attacks bounced off her shields but the defenses grew dimmer with each blow. Several green tendrils poked through the top of the headless bodies.

The half-Drow shoved her blade through Kenneth's flower and heart and the zombie thrashed wildly. The tendrils continued to grow and twine around each other where the head lay.

"Get away from the bloody thing so I can try something," Drysi shouted.

Alison yanked her blade out and jogged backward. The other witch threw her dagger and it struck the flower, exploded, and blew the top half of the body into several pieces.

Hana groaned. "This is both ridiculous and disgusting."

"All of you, protect Abigail!" Alison shouted. "I'll finish this. All of this."

She released her blade and focused energy into an explosive orb. Mason holstered his gun, hoisted the CEO, and threw her over his shoulder. She yelped as he rushed into the meeting hall. Hana and Drysi pelted after him.

The remaining Nereid zombie jerked forward, its movements more haphazard than when it had a head but not entirely random either.

So they must have some other way to see than simply borrowing eyes. That's fucking annoying.

Alison didn't have much time to ponder the nature of

plant zombies. Instead, she released her orb after the power had built for a few more seconds. It arced into the creature's chest and the zombie erupted. Whatever the flower had done to them seemed to weaken the overall integrity of the bodies.

She watched, her breath held, to see if they'd pull back together, but the pieces stopped twitching after about thirty seconds.

When she was finally satisfied that they presented no more danger, she grew wings and flew back to the plane and the seedpod. She charged an orb with even more power and incinerated the pod in the explosive blaze.

A quick scrutiny revealed no others and she returned to the meeting hall and stomped inside. Her team surrounded Abigail on all sides, their weapons at the ready. A thin layer of moisture covered all the Nereids.

Der advanced toward her. "Did you destroy the pod?"

"Yeah," she responded acidly, "and now, I think you owe us a few answers."

CHAPTER TWENTY-ONE

Der looked at the terrified Nereids and back to Alison. "Yes, we do."

"Then get to it," she responded. "A man's dead. A Nereid's dead. Our plane is a smoking wreck."

"The Curse Flower pods are part of a dark legacy, one that should have long been buried but stubbornly refuses to stay in the past. They are a hideous weapon, a corruption of the beauty of life and one that seeks to turn everything into more of itself." She approached Alison. "Before we talk, allow us to apply protective magic. The seeds don't last long when exposed to sunlight, but the Corrupted themselves are much sturdier and their claws can pass their corruption along."

"What about the seeds?"

"A single seed isn't enough to turn people, and our magic ensures that enough won't accumulate for corruption, even at night."

Alison looked at Mason, Hana, and Drysi. They all nodded their assent.

"Okay, do it," she ordered.

Der placed her hands on Alison's cheeks. They heated for a few seconds before lukewarm water spread and coated her body and hair. The odd warmth was slightly distracting but not painful. A few other Nereids placed the protective magic on the others. Now, everyone in the room looked like they had just stepped out of the ocean.

"We'll need to reapply this every day until we've cleansed the island," Der explained.

Alison narrowed her eyes. "Was this weapon created during the Great War?"

The Nereid shook her head. "Long after. It was created on Earth specifically to avoid the attention of those on Oriceran who might stop its creation." She released a weary sigh. "In the deep past, some of our ancestors were involved in that process, or at least in guarding the creation. Because it fails to corrupt creatures of the sea, we have reason to believe our kind might have been involved in its creation, but the truth is the reasons are lost to even us. Perhaps it was a bribe for some great perceived boon, or perhaps they suffered at the hands of others and wanted vengeance. There are many theories, but few truths left. What has come down to us is that a small group of our ancestors rebelled against the dark coalition who wanted to use the weapons but at a terrible cost."

Abigail shivered and rubbed her shoulders. "Worse than what we saw?"

"The remnants of the coalition were able to curse our ancestors with a particularly painful and mocking curse. The level of magic necessary to maintain their natural lives increased and the use of any portal would kill them." Der gestured around the room. "When the first ancestors regained the ocean, they hoped the curse would go with them, but it soon became clear that it wouldn't. Our sisterhood is forever denied Oriceran, and we were forced to remain here to stay alive. It's only since the gates have opened that any of us can survive off this island. But, in a sense, it didn't matter. The curse only reinforced what we already needed to do."

"What do you mean?" Alison asked.

"The Curse Flower pods were never fully destroyed." Der looked at the exit with a mournful expression. "And our ancestors realized what could happen if they were ever released into a city. Their curse is our curse. Their shame is our shame. It's our duty to ensure the Curse Flowers never spread beyond this island."

"But you could have asked for help," Hana observed. "If not before the gates opened, then after."

"We thought we didn't need help. We thought they were contained, with only a rare occurrence, but the previous mining company almost unearthed hundreds of them." Der scoffed. "They dug in an area where we had forbidden them to work. What I don't understand is why a seedpod was out now. I thought we had contained all of them."

Drysi paced, her face pale. She nodded to Ine. "Someone sliced her up, and it wasn't some damned plant zombie."

"I didn't see them," Ine replied. "It was all so quick. But she's right. It wasn't a Corrupted. I would have already been changed into one of them."

Abigail sank to the floor, pale and quiet.

I bet you never imagined this sort of shit when you estab-lished contact with the Nereids.

Mason looked at the CEO with concern before he returned his attention to Alison. "One of those things obviously blew the plane up, and I'm sure I'm not the only one who felt the magic when it happened."

Alison nodded grimly. "Which means the seedpod and the Corrupted aren't the cause of the trouble, they're merely a weapon." She sighed. "Abigail, how much do you know about the company who had the contract before? The Nereids won't have that kind of deep knowledge. Even if they used truth spells, the man who signed the contract might not have been the man who called the shots."

The other woman frowned in concentration. "They are known to cut corners, but other than a few fines here and there, there's been no serious legal action outside the occasional accidental death lawsuit. Why?"

"Because Der's right to be suspicious." The half-Drow nodded toward the Nereid. "And there might be someone else on this island causing trouble. Maybe the previous company wasn't what it appeared to be. I don't know. If someone else knew about the Curse Flowers, they might have thought they could get control of them if they took care of the Nereids first."

A murmur of fear swept through the room.

Drysi winced. "Bloody hell, Alison, and I thought I was paranoid."

Hana snorted. "You need to hang around Alison more. Although, in her defense, a lot of nasty assholes do plot against her."

Der sighed. "We must beg your assistance even further."

Alison gave her a hungry grin. "Oh, don't worry. We'll find the bastard and we'll make him pay."

"That's not what I'm talking about. You destroyed the seedpod, but I'm sure it had already released seeds."

"Something like that, yes—spores or seeds or particles. It definitely coughed them up."

The look of terror spread on the faces of the Nereids.

"Then we must cleanse the island over the next day," the leader explained. "We have powerful rituals that will allow us to purify the entire surface of the island, but it'll require most of our numbers. The very nature of the rituals brings the Corrupted, and if an enemy is lurking on the island, they might come as well. We need you to defend us while we perform the ritual."

"That's fine." Alison glanced at Abigail. "Right?"

The other woman nodded quickly and pushed to her feet. "Kenneth will have died for nothing if we don't stop this thing here and now."

The half-Drow shrugged. "We should get started right away, then. We'll arm up properly this time and we can end this nightmare."

Der shook her head and pointed to the ceiling, which was still ringed with light orbs. "The ritual requires the sun. We won't be able to perform it until tomorrow."

"So we have to wait around at night and hope zombies don't appear," Hana murmured. "That sounds like fun."

"The magic we used will protect you from corruption, but it won't repel them. They can still kill you."

"Then we'll fortify ourselves here in the meeting hall for the night," Alison suggested. "Forty-nine Nereids along with a witch, a wizard, and a Drow should be enough to secure one building."

Mason cleared his throat. "A, we still have to worry about someone else out there, and we also have to assume they're a magical."

"We can take guard shifts." She wandered toward the entrance and poked her head through. The wreckage still smoldered in the distance. "We should check that out further. We might be able to find some sort of clue."

He jogged toward the door. "I'll investigate it. You should set wards and protection glyphs up here."

Alison turned to Drysi and Hana. "You two grab all your gear from the huts. I'll wait here with the Nereids and Mason until you're back, then he can examine the wreckage while Drysi and I set wards up and Hana patrols the perimeter."

Abigail sighed. "Is there anything I can do?"

"The fact that you're calm is damned helpful as is." Alison offered her a confident smile. "Don't worry. I can't say I've ever fought plant zombies before, but I have fought a Mountain Strider and stopped it. No one else will die here."

And I damn well mean it.

———

Alison had barely finished setting up another ward when Mason returned from his trip to the wreckage, a deep frown on his face.

"Did you find something?" she asked and honestly hoped he'd say no.

He held a cellphone up. "I found this. It's Kenneth's."

She blinked. "It survived the explosion?"

"Yes." The bodyguard lowered the phone. "It's a little damaged, but it's surprisingly tough."

Alison shook her head in disbelief.

"I didn't exactly have Tahir to go through this thing," Mason continued his eyes downcast. "I checked the messages and stuff, though, to be thorough. Most of it is normal crap, but he had a number of articles open about the Friends of Carlyle and New Veil."

"Are you saying Kenneth was New Veil?" she asked.

"I'm saying it's a possibility."

Drysi, who sat in a corner and double-checked her enchanted knives, looked up. "New Veil? Why would a member of New Veil work for someone like her?" She nodded toward Abigail.

The CEO's face reddened and she shook her head. "I've known Kenneth for ten years. He's never expressed any sympathy for terrorists, let alone anti-magic terrorists. It's not as if he could have predicted ten years ago that he'd end up on an island like this. I didn't even know about the pods, so how could he?"

Alison walked to the entrance and stared at the stars. Despite all the horror, it was hard not to appreciate the clear night sky, untouched by the light pollution of human cities. Paradise had been turned into hell, however, and someone was responsible.

"It could be a coincidence," she mused. "He might have simply been curious about New Veil, but if he was a member, that would explain the plane and what happened to Ine."

Drysi began sliding her knives into various sheaths beneath her jacket. She'd retrieved the harness from the hut earlier. "And you're saying he blew himself up?"

"New Veil are fanatics," Alison insisted. "They might be willing to sacrifice themselves if they thought they could poison an entire island of magicals and stop anyone from getting the valuable magically charged mineral on it. New Veil might hate magic, but they're also willing to use artifacts. That might be how he surprised Ine."

Der scoffed. "Does it make a difference? The man's dead, whether he was a killer or not."

Abigail sighed and looked down.

I hate to have to go over this in front of her, but we have no choice.

"If Kenneth was the man behind all this and he's dead, that means we don't have someone else out there. But if he's not the man responsible, there's someone else out there who knows about the Curse Flowers. There's no way a flower simply happened to end up on the runway." She rubbed her chin and paced in frustration. "But how the hell would New Veil know about the flowers?"

Hana sighed as she stepped back into the meeting hall, her sword belt on. She'd passed by the entrance as part of her perimeter patrol and heard the last comment. "We have to defend the Nereids during the ritual, right? We'll find out then. If there's someone else involved, they'll show up."

"You're right. We should get some rest now." Alison pointed to the fox. "You and Mason take first watch. Drysi and I will take the second watch." She turned to Der. "And as long as we protect you, you can end this?"

"Yes," the Nereid insisted. "I swear upon my fallen sister."

"Then we'll do exactly that."

Alison stood outside and stared at the moon. Last she heard from the news, they'd made decent progress on Tranquility City, a moon base, using specially reinforced portals to help transport materials from Earth. The problem was that despite all the magical energy that flowed back into Earth from the gates, the actual level of magic rapidly grew weaker the farther you moved from Earth, even to a place as relatively close as the moon.

The early post-gate dreams of using magic to probe the entire Solar System or even explore the galaxy had run into harsh reality, but at least the world might get a moon base out of it.

The Nereids all lay huddled together and slumbered peacefully. Mason and Hana slept, their heads down on the center table.

Drysi stepped out of the meeting hall. The moonlight reflected off the Nereid moisture on her skin and gave her an ethereal glow. "It's not safe to be beyond the wards," she murmured. "Someone could ambush you out here."

Alison chuckled and turned, her smile gone. "I'm sorry. I know it's bullshit that I brought you on a job and claimed it would be a vacation and now, we're dealing with plant zombies."

The Welsh witch snorted. "You used to do bounties. You know how often those get fucked up. You have nothing to apologize for. While it's not my idea of a bloody fun time, I've been through worse."

"Worse than plant zombies and deadly magically-contaminated seeds?" She laughed. "If that's true, we've both led terrible lives."

Drysi threw a hand over her mouth to stifle her bark of laughter. She lowered her hand and smiled. "Yes, we need right and proper real jobs that don't involve dark wizards, bounties, or zombies." She inclined her head toward the plane wreckage. Wisps of dark gray smoke lingered over the area but the fires had long since gone out. "Do you think that poor bastard really was New Veil?"

"I don't know." Alison frowned, still unsettled by the question. "Here's the thing. I might be new at running a company, but I've dealt with people trying to kill me for half my life. I won't say I have a sixth sense or anything, but I trust my instincts."

"And what do your instincts tell you?"

"That even if Kenneth was New Veil, he wasn't the only threat—and I'm not talking about the Corrupted."

Drysi's mouth twitched and she shook her arms out. "That sent chills right through me, but there are four of us and one of him, and that's if we don't count the Nereids."

She nodded. "That's what I'm counting on." She folded her arms and looked at the moon once more.

They'd find the truth out soon enough.

CHAPTER TWENTY-TWO

The Nereids formed concentric circles on the beach and Alison frowned as she watched them. She'd spread her small team in a rough semi-circle around the nymphs, but it wasn't the most defensible formation, even if they only had to protect three sides. Water animals were immune to the Curse Flower, according to Der. Their enemies would likely come from the forest, especially since no one had seen anything since the group had risen at dawn to prepare for the ritual.

The leader insisted the ritual required the Nereids to be close to the ocean, under the sky, and touching the ground with their bare feet, something that eliminated any ability Alison and her team had to easily fortify the position.

Sometimes, magic is really fucking annoying. Why can't they have some reinforced stone ritual fortress with massive walls, towers, and railgun turrets to shoot plant zombies with? If the Corrupted get through on any side, we might be screwed.

Der had explained that the ritual could succeed even if they lost Nereids but losing more people to this bizarre plant zombie plague wasn't acceptable. Whether it was Kenneth or someone else behind it didn't matter for the moment. Their immediate enemy was the Corrupted, not New Veil or any dangerous wizards.

Ine and a few other Nereids hurried toward the beach to join their sisters. They'd needed to retrieve a few ritual shell necklaces from their homes. The remaining nymphs filtered into the circle and murmured quietly to the others.

Abigail stood on the far side. Alison refused to allow her to be involved in the fight, but if the Corrupted made it through both the Brownstone team, she would die anyway.

The half-Drow layered light and shadow magic into a thick sandwich of shields. She didn't bother with a shadow blade yet. For the initial defense, she wanted to concentrate on pure explosive magic. She would worry about a blade when the monsters were too close to risk the attacks.

Mason surveyed the area, his wand out. "Of course, we have to end up with a bunch of assholes that I can't deal with in hand-to-hand. Fighting plant zombies with my least favorite spells...what a terrible morning date you've arranged, A."

She snorted. "Technically, you're the one who brought us this job."

He laughed. "True enough."

"I can't even risk my claws," Hana pointed out. Her tails waved in the wind and her vulpine eyes narrowed at the trees in the distance as she tapped the crystal ring on her hand three times. Her skin immediately turned red. Even if she couldn't risk using her claws against the Corrupted, her fox speed would help. She patted the *tachi*. "I'll try to concentrate on at least slowing them down with gun and sword while you three do your thing and blow them back to hell. But now, I wish I brought a few more grenades along."

Is that what we should do on every job from now on? Assume maximum possible risk and bring heavy ordnance? I'm normally enough to win against most people, though. It just so happens that a cursed plant zombie horde works against my strength.

No wonder Mom and Dad always bitched about zombies.

Drysi smiled. "I'm looking forward to it. It's easier when you don't have to worry about anything and merely blow the bloody bastards away. No worries about bounty status or if I might damage some building, so I can go full strength on them." She slammed her fist into her palm. "If there's some other bastard behind this later, that's only more fun."

"I'm glad you're enjoying it," Alison replied.

Several seagulls passed high overhead.

They're trapped on this island by the storm. Does that mean there are more of them around here, then?

Der raised a conch to her lips and blew hard, the sound mournful. The Nereids all raised their arms and chanted, and their melodious voices weaved together in eerie harmony. Waves of magic washed over Alison.

"Remember, we can't let any of the Corrupted through," she explained. "The Nereids' have the anti-corruption spell, but they can't have any shield spells up during the ritual. Anything that gets through will shred them."

Hana, Drysi, and Mason all nodded.

The conch sounded again, and the Nereids spoke faster and louder. The magic continued to build.

Dark shadows rushed toward the beach from the tree line—dozens on the ground and dozens in the air.

"So much for us getting lucky," Alison muttered. She channeled energy into an explosive orb.

Mason immediately launched fireballs with his wand. Drysi didn't throw a knife right away but instead, drew her gun and fired at the aerial creatures that approached rapidly. Hana took the hint and released a volley with her 9mm as well.

The circles of Nereids now moved in different directions and their chants altered depending on their position. Blue light pulsed from the nymphs and swept over the island. The Corrupted slowed, which allowed the Brownstone team to pick off several and punch holes in the enemy line.

Alison released her first orb after a lengthy charging period. The bright magical energy hurtled free from her and erupted into the closest Corrupted—what once had most likely been some sort of wild goat. A massive explosion decimated the creature and a few others nearby, and while it did enough damage to finish several off, those farther away were merely singed.

The air itself now seemed to sing in harmony with the changing Nereids as the blue pulses increased in frequency and swept the island. Several of the Corrupted stopped and twitched.

We can do this.

Another mob of animals emerged from the forest.

"Oh, come on!" Alison shouted in protest.

She threw several quick explosive bolts to annihilate a corrupted badger and a swarm of field mice. Hana and

Drysi swept another wave of birds aside. Their attacks didn't kill them, but at least they would now only face enemies on the ground in the immediate future.

The survivors of the first wave were less than ten yards away from the Brownstone defensive line now. Hana holstered her gun and yanked her *tachi* out.

Drysi threw two explosive knives in rapid succession and the force of them cut down a wave of vermin. A trio of scorched wild cats survived the assault and continued their approach.

Alison extended a shadow blade from her left hand while she continued to hurl explosive bolts with her other. Her heart pounded and her breathing became a little labored. As powerful as she was, even she didn't have unlimited magic.

A new group of creatures emerged from the forest.

What the hell is that?

An eight-legged monster approached their line. Somehow, two wild goats had been fused together by the Curse Flower. They were now covered with not only the plant corruption but a series of sharp barbs all over their bodies.

Another pulse from the Nereids slowed the attacking animals. The half-Drow used the opportunity to launch a barrage of magic bolts and orbs at the eight-legged Corrupted. A few fireballs from Mason helped to finish the beast off. The entire first wave of assailants had been defeated, but the second and third waves hadn't taken much damage as the security team had focused on the immediate threat.

Several more tangled combinations of animals

approached the beach, including new plant beasts with six, eight, and even twelve legs in one case.

Why are there suddenly so many more fusions?

Her question was answered when a pulse from the ritual struck the line and two corrupted goats fused together.

Damn it. That's annoying, but if the ritual didn't slow them on occasion, we'd already be overrun. Note to self, next time we go to a remote island, pack a few big machine guns.

The Brownstone team continued to offer destruction and death as they thinned the approaching monster horde. Drysi gritted her teeth as she tossed her last explosive knife. She retrieved her wand and generated a stream of fireballs.

The Nereids' voices now drowned everything else out. Their movement quickened and their arms were still raised in the air.

Hana slashed a six-legged monstrosity in half. "I'm dry when it comes to bullets, by the way." She continued to chop at the creature until it lay in three times as many pieces as it had legs.

Mason kicked a badger-goat fusion away before he obliterated it at point-blank range with a fireball that knocked the wizard back a few feet.

Alison's explosive bolts had carved a path through the writhing mass of animals.

It'd be nice if they finished the ritual sooner than later.

A tangled mass of legs and barbs sprinted to her side and charged Drysi, who had been focused on an attacking flyer. The Corrupted barreled into the Welsh bounty hunter and she tumbled hard. The monster surged to trample her. The attacks bounced off her shield but drew closer and closer to the Welsh witches' head.

Alison hurtled forward and fired a few quick blasts to distract the creature. They had little effect in terms of real damage, but the beast turned its attention away from the fallen woman. The half-Drow followed through with a throaty challenge and slashed it in half with her shadow blade.

The dismembered fragments thrashed and Drysi rolled away. Alison delivered another three explosive charges.

The woman scrambled to her feet and resumed her magical assault. "Damn, that was bloody close."

Another minute passed as the increasingly twisted Corrupted tried to pierce their line. The Nereids ended their chant with a single loud shout. Bright, blinding blue light suffused the entire area, almost eye-searing in its intensity.

Alison stumbled backward and hurled a few explosive bolts in the general direction of the forest line. She blinked a few times until her vision cleared.

All the Corrupted lay dead on the ground but now, the Curse Flowers and corrupted plant matter flaked off and turned gray.

The Nereids were all on their knees, their breathing ragged.

Der raised the conch and blew it again. "My sisters, we have cleansed the island, and for the first time since we've conducted this ritual, we lost no other sisters."

Alison released her shadow blade and shield and took a deep breath. "Is everyone okay?"

It was only the monsters. No wizard or anyone else showed

up. Kenneth must have been behind it after all. He must have wanted to make sure we didn't have a chance to escape and that we'd be dead before someone could rescue us from the mainland.

She glanced at Abigail. The woman looked relieved.

There's no reason to talk to her about it right now. He's already dead.

Hana sheathed her sword and turned toward Alison to offer her a thumbs-up. Her tails swayed in the light ocean breeze. "Let's never do that again, okay? That seriously sucked in every way."

Mason slipped his wand back into his holster. "I'm only glad we don't have to clean this mess up."

Alison nodded as she looked around at all the dead animals. Had one brief seedpod really created so many Corrupted?

Drysi walked over to her and stuck her hand out. "Damn, Alison, I can't say that was a tidy fight, but you saved my life again. Depending on how you count, this is the third time."

She shook her hand. "We watch each other's back at Brownstone Security."

I hope it's finally over. I'll never, ever convince myself that a job will be easy ever again.

CHAPTER TWENTY-THREE

Alison's stomach rumbled as she munched on some berries in the meeting hall. She sat at a table with Mason and reflected on the strange battle. Hana and Drysi rested in one of the huts. They'd earned it, and only her busy mind wouldn't let her sleep.

Abigail spoke quietly with Der in a far corner, but most of the other Nereids worked on burying the animals outside to return their nutrients to the soil. It wasn't as difficult a task as it might be with the help of magic, although it was definitely grim.

"She'll still try to mine the aventurine, won't she?" the half-Drow asked.

Mason nodded. "From what she mentioned, yes. Abigail told me that since the truth is out now, it'll be easy to work with the Nereids. Aeternum might even be able to bring additional equipment to help track areas where there are greater concentrations of seedpods. She'll also coordinate with the EU and UN about the issue. I don't know if they can get rid of them totally, but they could reduce the numbers."

Alison nodded. "I talked with Der a little after the ritual. The Nereids have purified the island countless times, but new seedpods always form." She frowned.

"I know that look. What's bothering you, A?"

"Kenneth."

He shrugged. "Given what we found on his phone, I think he recently started thinking the New Veil was right. He might have worked for Abigail, but his job didn't involve magic."

"That's not what's bothering me." She leaned toward him to whisper. "If he was New Veil and blew the plane up to strand us here while he released the seedpod, why not blow the plane up when we were halfway here? None of us were shielded on the flight. He could easily have killed the Dark Princess, the woman who took down Scott Carlyle."

"Maybe he didn't want to kill Abigail, too," he whispered in response.

"But he'd help flood an island with plant zombies that would kill her?" She scoffed. "And that's the other thing. The only reason the Nereids admitted anything to us about the Curse Flowers was because we already saw them in action. There's no way some random New Veil terrorist would know about them. Abigail didn't know about them, so it's not like he picked up on it second-hand."

Mason frowned. "If there was someone else involved, they would have attacked during the ritual, right?"

Alison ran her hands through her hair. She wondered if stress could turn a Drow's hair black. "And that's why this drives me crazy. I've missed something and I feel like it's right in front of me. But—"

The building shook so violently that some of the figurines fell off the wall.

Her stomach lurched as one of the most massive waves of magic she'd ever felt passed through her. The beautiful clear skies vanished in an instant. Laden, dark-gray clouds appeared overheard and peals of thunder followed the earthquake.

"Did someone schedule the Apocalypse when I wasn't paying attention?" Alison blinked.

Der ran outside the meeting hall and looked off into the distance. Abigail followed and several other Nereids ran toward them and stared in the same direction.

Alison and Mason jogged outside to see what everyone was looking at. A bright line shone from the side of one of the central mountain peaks on the island. Heavy winds blew curtains of rain across the island. Several massive bolts of lightning struck in the forest.

Shit. If that keeps up, half this island will catch on fire, even with this crazy rain.

Hana hurried out of one of the huts and ran toward her. "What the hell is going on?"

Der pointed to the mountain. "It's the trident."

"The trident?" The half-Drow frowned. "What trident?"

"An ancient artifact. It's how we generate the storm. That light is shining exactly where it's located." The Nereid looked at the ground, her eyes filled with pain. "It's as if all our ancestors' sins have returned at once to punish us."

Alison had wondered how they'd managed the storm, even with the special aventurine supply. The magic she'd seen from the Nereids, even their purification ritual, wasn't anywhere near that scale. They'd mentioned an artifact but not the nature of, and she'd not had time to satisfy her curiosity—of they'd been willing to provide details, which was debatable.

The gargantuan magical fluctuations that rippled through the air made her shudder. Several Nereids fell to their knees and vomited.

Mason pinched the bridge of his nose. "Fuck."

Der pointed toward the mountain. "You can fly, Alison. I don't know why this is happening, but you have to stop the trident. None of us can get there quickly enough."

She stared at the woman like she'd asked her to box the Fremont Troll without magic. "How? I don't know anything about the trident, or what kind of binding glyphs, rituals, or wards might even work to deactivate it."

The woman rattled off an incantation in a language Alison didn't recognize. "Grasp the trident and say that incantation."

Alison repeated it.

Der nodded and raised her hand. Water pooled in the center and receded to reveal a small pearl. "If you can't stop it with the incantation, throw this at the trident and it will be destroyed."

Several nearby Nereids gasped.

The ground shuddered violently once more and another massive lightning bolt struck nearby to scatter dirt and sand near the airstrip. The wind howled.

"We have no choice," the leader shouted over the noise. "None of us can get there in time, and it's out of control. If we don't do this, the entire island might be destroyed but the dark legacy will remain. The danger will remain." She gestured to the meeting hall. "We'll take shelter and raise a shield to protect what we can."

Alison took the offered pearl and nodded to Mason and Hana. "Keep Abigail safe."

Other Nereids streamed in from the forest and the beach. All headed toward the meeting hall and strained against the heavy winds and rain.

She extended her wings. "Go wake Drysi's comatose butt and get her in there to help shield the meeting hall." She took a few deep breaths and summoned a shield. With the pearl clutched tightly in her hand, she pushed upward and strained to advance through the buffeting winds.

What will happen if I am struck by one of those lightning bolts? They're not exactly normal.

All the more reason not to waste time, she realized. She gritted her teeth, funneled more power into her wings, and forced her way forward toward the shining trident on the mountain. After a short distance, she generated a small wall of air a few inches away from her face to at least provide a few inches of visibility without rain. The trident continued to glow brighter with each passing minute.

Two lightning bolts crackled near her and her heart rate kicked up.

It's too bad I can't open a portal—and that the Nereid could use one. I could then at least evacuate everyone somewhere safe, but it's not useful to worry about shit that won't happen for decades when I probably have minutes to solve the problem.

As Alison grew closer to the trident, she frowned. A shimmering dome encased the bright artifact embedded into a small ledge and the rain bounced off it to confirm its effectiveness. She descended toward it, unsure if she'd be able to penetrate, but she eased through the barrier without difficulty. Perhaps it was a life-sensitive barrier.

She slowed and hovered in one place. While she had to shield her eyes because of the bright artifact, the dome sheltered the small section of the mountain from the storm as effectively as thick walls.

Alison released her wings and descended to the ledge. She cast a quick spell to filter some of the light from her eyes. Her vision clearer, she headed toward the trident but leapt back at a sudden movement from the corner of her eye. A water whip snaked into her and knocked her down the mountain, but a quick shadow line pulled her up.

She kept one hand clutched around the pearl and turned in the direction of the earlier movement. Ine stood off to the side of the trident, her frown intense and disapproving.

"You shouldn't be here," the Nereid said accusingly. She fingered an aventurine necklace—the first jewelry Alison had seen any of the nymphs wear.

Is that some sort of artifact?

"Did you just fucking attack me?" Alison demanded, now out of patience. "I'm trying to deactivate the trident."

Ine shook her head. "It's too late now. There's not enough time."

"I have the pearl from Der."

The Nereid's breath caught and she held her hand out. "Give it to me."

You're too fucking eager. Too fucking eager by far.

Alison layered another shield over herself and summoned a shadow blade. She tightened her grasp around the pearl in her other hand. "It was you all along, wasn't it? There was no mysterious shadow man. You cut yourself and what—blew the plane up, too?"

Ine's lip quivered. "You don't understand what it's like. There's no future here. Time stopped thousands of years ago. They won't allow us to have a future because of something Nereids did thousands of years before we were born? It's unfair. The island needed to be made unsafe. It was the only way to regain a future." She released a nervous laugh. "Then the humans can come in and drop their nuclear bombs or their wizards could use the magic even King Oriceran fears. It's as you said before. We don't have to live here. A kemana perhaps—anything—but I knew my sisters would never leave, not unless they were forced to."

"Are you fucking insane? You could have killed them. Now, you will still kill them." Alison pointed her blade at the trident that grew steadily brighter. Even her dimming spell strained against it and the glare highlighted the Nereid in stark clarity. "Now, let me past you."

Ine raised her arms and two loose water whips appeared. "I thought, when the gates finally opened, we would be free, but no, they still insisted that we stay. I tried to talk to others, but everyone talked of duty and the dark legacy. How long did we intend to wait? Our sisterhood had already waited thousands of years. Would five thousand years pass and another of my sisters be born like me? Reflecting and craving for a world she could never know?"

"I'm sure we can work something out," Alison stated calmly, "but we have to take care of that trident. This isn't the way."

"No. There are no options left. This is the only way."

She sighed. "Then I'll have to go through you, I'm afraid. You have your reasons. Fine. But your little Curse Flower stunt cost another Nereid her life and bombing the plane killed an innocent man." She shook her head. "You won't be able to defeat me. Trust me on this."

"I don't need to win. I simply need to stall you long enough." Ine's gaze raised and her face scrunched in confusion. After a few seconds, she looked at Alison once more. "And I can win. This close to the trident, I can draw its power through the necklace. I prepared this, too—slowly, even though it's dangerous. I needed to make sure I could fight my sisters off if they understood what I had planned."

A shadow passed over Alison and she spun instinctively.

Drysi hovered over her. She held a glowing umbrella in one hand and aimed her pistol at Alison with the other. "Look at me, I'm the Welsh Mary Poppins. I never thought I'd need to use this thing, but here we are. I'm glad I packed it." She gestured with the gun. "It's loaded with anti-magic bullets that I've further enchanted. At this range, even you wouldn't survive if I put a few into your head."

"What the hell is going on, Drysi?" she asked.

The mountain shuddered with a violent tremor as the bounty hunter floated to the ground. "You're a better woman than I am, Alison Brownstone, but I still have to do this."

Alison turned to keep both the Nereid and Drysi in her peripheral vision. "Do what, exactly? Did Ine pay you off somehow?"

"No, I intended to kill you for some time, but I needed to find the right time and place to do it tidy-like, you see, when there'd be no evidence to point at me. Basically, with no one around to look for vengeance." The witch sighed. "I thought I might have a chance while fighting the Corrupted, but there were too many of the bloody things. Still, there are a goodly number of dark wizards who need you dead." She shook her head. "When I saw you fly away into the storm, I knew I had my chance. It was unpleasant getting here and avoiding notice, I can tell you that, and I don't care why the Nereid is doing what she's doing. We'll both have secrets we can keep now, won't we?"

The half-Drow gritted her teeth. "Everyone on this island will die if I don't take care of that trident. If you want to kill me for the dark families, fine, but at least let me save the Nereids and my friends. It doesn't benefit the families to kill everyone on this island. You can't be a lord without peasants, right?"

"This dome will protect us," Ine announced. "Not everyone will die. Once it's done its work, it's simply a matter of bleeding the energy off. Perhaps I'll sell it when I leave this place."

Drysi's eyes narrowed. "That's who you're concerned about right now, Alison? Everyone else? You're the one who will die. It's your fault. You shouldn't have interfered with the families. They wouldn't have targeted you if you hadn't, but you couldn't leave well enough alone."

Alison moved to slip the pearl into her pocket. Ine struck at her with a massive water whip. She spun instinctively and raised her hand to throw a spell before she realized she'd opened the hand with the pearl. The Nereid grinned and slapped at it with the water whip to send it bouncing down the side of the mountain.

Ine stared after it, a satisfied smile on her face.

The half-Drow drew a deep breath. "If you're going to shoot me, Drysi, do it, because otherwise, I'll dispose of this bitch and find a way to stop the artifact."

The witch stared at her for several seconds and raised her gun. "Sorry about this. I have to pay back the debts I owe."

Alison narrowed her eyes and crouched, ready to strike.

Drysi pulled the trigger quickly three times and Ine screamed and stumbled back. Blue blood poured from wounds in her neck and chest.

The Nereid coughed blood and tumbled over the side of the ledge. She bounced and rolled down the mountain and finally vanished into the darkness of the storm.

The bounty hunter holstered her pistol. "What a crazy bitch."

CHAPTER TWENTY-FOUR

A lison stared at Drysi, her shields and blade still active. "You work for the dark families?"

"I've been a traitorous bloody bitch this entire time," the woman announced. "You don't understand. I don't work for the dark families. My family *is* a dark family. Well, was. I'm the last after dwindling generations. We used to have pride, wealth, and status, and that legacy is gone, squandered by the idiots I'm descended from. I'm the last one in my line, and I intend—intended—to do something about it."

She scoffed. "That's what this is all about? Pride, wealth, and status? Thousands of people could have died in Seattle, and that's only one example and ignores all the people who have been killed by dark wizard schemes."

Drysi pointed at the bright trident. "You can yell at me, or we can stop that thing."

Alison eyed her suspiciously. "How do I know this isn't a trick?"

"You don't, but I already had opportunities to kill you

and I didn't. If I wanted to kill you or do the bidding of the others, I would have shot you instead of Ine." The witch drew her gun slowly and then tossed it over the ledge. "We both know I don't stand much of a chance against you when it comes to a straight-up magical fight."

Even as the dome prevented the crackle and fury of the storm from fully registering, the bright flashes and dense rain all around them reminded Alison that it had worsened considerably. The Nereids and her friends probably protected themselves by combining their magic, but no one could hold out forever against such intensity.

Alison edged toward the trident. Even if she didn't have the pearl, there had to be something she could do. "And why didn't you try and kill me, especially when I was distracted?"

"Because of family pride," Drysi confessed, her face tight. "My reward for getting rid of you was supposed to help to restore the honor and status of my family among the dark families, but I've decided the cost is too high. You've saved my life more than once, and I plan to kill you?" She shook her head. "It doesn't make any bloody sense."

"There are a lot of things about dark wizards that don't make sense."

The woman frowned. "And you're not what they think you are. I know that because I've worked closely with you."

"Meaning what?" She strengthened the light filter spell and tried to take hold of the trident. It burned the tips of her fingers even through her shields and she hissed in pain.

Shit. If I can't do it directly, I'll have to manipulate it magically somehow. But how?

"They think you're like them." Drysi scoffed and squinted as she approached the artifact. She threw the umbrella down and drew her wand. "I'm protecting my eyes." She turned and muttered a quick spell before she turned once more. "They don't understand you because they think you want their power and position, but you don't. You only want to use your power to protect others, which is allegedly what we're supposed to do among the families by establishing an order in which they rule. The idea is that we'll protect people overall with our actions."

Alison's laugh was loudly mocking. "Excuse me if I say that's fucking deluded. Assassinations, murders, and terrorism don't lead to a better world. If the dark families want to rule, they should prove they're worthy of it, and so far, that's a big fucking negative. The world won't become what a bunch of arrogant assholes want simply because they keep murdering people."

Drysi's face tightened and she didn't reply.

The half-Drow waved a hand dismissively. "I don't have time for your self-serving bullshit right now. I have to deactivate this thing. Wait. I almost forgot."

She shouted the incantation. Nothing happened. She tried again and exactly the same thing happened—nothing.

"Damn it," she yelled.

If I had a whole group of magicals with me, we could do some sort of ritual, but I can't fly all the Nereids and everyone else up in the middle of the storm.

Alison attempted a quick dampening spell and grimaced as more energy crackled over the trident.

"Bleed," Drysi suggested. "It's probably our only chance."

"Huh? What now? If you want to cut me, go ahead and try." She released the shadow blade. There were far more pressing concerns than dark family assassins, whether they struggled with their conscience or not. "But I don't think that'll do anything to help anyone else."

"No, it's what Ine said. She intended to bleed the energy off, probably with the necklace." The witch raised her wand and made a show of pointing it at the trident but not Alison. "Maybe if we bleed enough energy off, you can disable it. It's a powerful artifact, but it's still only an artifact in the end."

Huh. Color me damned surprised.

"That might actually be true." Alison shot a sidelong glance at the other woman. "Right now, there's too much raw energy flowing through it to even try to reach it." She considered the plan. "It couldn't hurt. I can't even touch the damned thing, so it's not like I can fly it away. But if we can bring the power level down to somewhere in the neighborhood of more manageable, I could use some sort of binding spell—at least until Der could come up and examine it. This is an artifact, not a lifeform, so in theory, it should be somewhat easier than what I did with the Troll. It won't be stable, but it's at least a possibility."

The line between desperation and brilliance could be very thin. She wasn't sure if they hadn't already vaulted over that line with their plan.

Committed and with no other options, she took several deep breaths and raised her hands. She attempted to draw on the energy radiating from the trident and tried to feel out the unique texture. Fire ran through her veins, and the small number of berries in her stomach threatened to come up.

"Shit," she muttered. "It's already too much. Trying to bleed energy off will kill me."

Drysi looked disappointed. "So, even Alison Brownstone fears death in the end?"

"I can't bind the damned thing if I'm dead," Alison countered. "Maybe we could blow the entire ledge and try to carry it to the ocean somehow without touching the trident?"

The bounty hunter nodded to the storm outside the dome. "We don't have time for that. Are you saying the problem is that you can't bleed the energy off, survive, and do the binding spell?"

Alison circled the trident, her dimming spell once again challenged to the point where she had to squint. "If I could shunt energy away for perhaps a half a minute, that might be enough time. But I can't do both. I'd pass out toward the end. It might not be a ritual that requires dozens of Nereids, but it's also not a matter where I simply shout an incantation and wave my hand either."

Drysi nodded and shook her wand. "I think I can tap into the energy. All I have to do is not die for a while, right?"

"You don't understand. If you do this, you'll still force way more magical energy through your system than you could handle. I should know. It hurt me, and my baseline levels are already damned high."

"It must be good to be a Drow princess and have all that power handed to you." The Welsh witch pointed her wand at the trident. "But none of that changes what I need to do. Well, princess, it's time for one last job together. I might not be from a royal line, but I'm from a line that has done great things in the past, whether you think that's worthy of respect or not."

"Are you're serious about this?"

She nodded. "If it's time for the Jones line to die off, then it'll die off with honor. I won't assassinate the woman who has saved my life multiple times without thought of reward and who cared more about me than my alleged allies. I don't think I can pull off the kind of binding spell you're talking about anyway. So I'm the logical choice to try to handle the energy. I might fail, but I don't think so. This is all dependent on you being able to do what you say."

"If you can bring the energy down, I'll bind the artifact." Alison stared at the woman for a few seconds before she nodded slowly. "Okay, then. We both know what we need to do."

Several violent lightning strikes nearby made Alison wonder how loud and overwhelming the storm was for everyone outside the dome.

Where the hell is this dome from? The trident itself? It must be.

Drysi held nothing but pain and weariness in her eyes. "Let's do this before the storm takes everyone out. But there's one last thing you should know in case you make it but I don't."

"And what's that?"

"Conrad Barnes. He's the man I worked for. He's English, lives in London, and leads a group in the dark families called the Seventh Order."

Alison nodded. "I know about the Seventh Order."

"You do?"

"I know they exist but I didn't know any of their leaders."

"Anyway, he has some kind of plan for Seattle," the woman explained and confirmed Izzie's earlier information. "His plan for me here was simple. I assassinate you and scuttle the deal so he could swoop in with his own company and gain the magical aventurine for his own plans." Drysi chuckled. "When that plane exploded, I thought he'd somehow sent someone else in to finish the job. It turns out the Nereid constantly handed me opportunities that I wouldn't allow myself to follow through on, but now, I'll choose the kind of person I want to be."

The half-Drow nodded quickly. "We'll save everyone if we work together. Let's show this damned trident who the two baddest bitches on this island are."

"Bloody right we will." The witch shouted an incantation. A crackling line of energy surged from the trident toward her wand and split off in several directions. The shifting, irregular lines scorched the rock and seared the dirt on the ledge. She fell to one knee and grimaced in pain.

She's giving me the chance. Now, I have to do my part.

Alison reached out to the trident again with a spell. The power was still too much and pain suffused her body. As the seconds ticked away, Drysi coughed blood and her body shuddered with her effort to retain control.

The trident began to dim.

She's actually pulling it off.

Encouraged, she motioned carefully with her hand and

followed this with the practiced incantation. The effort produced a few glowing symbols to hover over the trident. Ignoring her pain, she drew on all her education and training, including at the School of Necessary Magic and with Myna and the other Drow.

Sometimes, you have to do something clever and sometimes, you need to risk a little shock and pull the plug.

Drysi slumped forward but maintained a tight grip on her wand with both hands. Energy continued to flow from the artifact to the wand and out. Alison persisted with the binding spell. Fiery pain shot through her body from the intense power that flowed and pulsed, even with the witch doing her best to draw the magic off.

Blood leaked from Drysi's mouth and eyes. She wouldn't last much longer.

She's not a good person, Alison thought. *She worked for the dark families and who knows what sort of things they had her help with? This isn't like Myna. This isn't a sacrifice for me. This is penance.*

But everyone should always have one last chance.

Alison persisted doggedly with the binding spell, despite her own pain. Drysi now lay flat on her stomach, her breathing shallow and her eyes closed, but she clutched her wand above her head and the energy channeling continued.

I'm out of time. She can't last, and I don't have time to do this smoothly. It's time to roll the dice.

"Sorry, Drysi," she said regretfully. "What I'm about to do will probably kill us both, but if it makes you feel any better, we have a decent chance to save the Nereids and the others. Not that it's the thing with the highest odds of happening."

"And what's the thing with the highest odds of happening?" the bounty hunter muttered, her cheek against the hard rock of the ledge.

"Oh, nothing special. In that situation, the trident explodes and kills us anyway."

She managed a pained chuckle. "No pressure, then. I've not got...much...left...in...me."

The half-Drow dragged in a deep breath. She combined shadow and light magic carefully before she whispered another incantation. The trident brightened again and almost blinded her despite her existing vision spell. A shockwave catapulted them both away from the artifact and their shields ripped off.

Drysi moaned and pitched over the side of the ledge, her eyes closed, and her wand slipped from her grip.

Alison's vision cleared, and she scrambled to the edge of the ledge in time to see the other witch bounce off the side of the mountain and disappear into the darkness of the trees below. The trident pulsed a few times and dimmed with each silent throb and the intensity and frequency of the lightning decreased.

Several more surges followed with longer intervals between. The clouds began to part, and the last few bolts of lightning crackled harmlessly before sunshine broke through.

She moved as close to the side of the ledge as she dared and searched for any sign of Drysi but saw nothing but the mountain and trees below. If the witch had fallen that far in that condition, there was no way she could have survived.

Weary beyond belief, she sighed and sat beside the trident.

I don't know how to feel about that, but at least she did the right thing in the end.

CHAPTER TWENTY-FIVE

Once she had recovered some of her strength, Alison flew back to the village. Although the storm had abated and the main threat was gone, the status quo had not reset. Several of the buildings were burned husks. In other cases, walls and roofs had been torn away, if not the entire structure, leaving only jagged remnants and the meager belongings strewn along the beach. Smoke rose from different parts of the forest, although the residual dampness from the earlier torrential rainfall kept the surprisingly small number of fires contained.

Nereids wandered the village and beach to inspect the damage and most looked stunned at what their protective artifact had wrought.

I don't know how they should look at it. They had the bad luck that a crazy Nereid almost obliterated them all, but on the other hand, most of them survived.

She winced. They hadn't witnessed what happened on the mountain, which meant she still had to break the news about Ine.

That will be fun, but it can wait a few minutes.

Hana and Mason stood outside the village meeting hall, one of the few buildings completely untouched.

All their shielding worked.

Hana waved her arms at her until she landed. The fox gave her a thumbs-up. "Good job. Not that I ever doubted you."

"Is everyone okay?" Alison asked and gestured to a nearby blackened hut missing half its walls. "This place doesn't look so great."

Mason nodded at the meeting hall. "It got tough at times, but we held the defenses. I'm glad it all ended when it did, though." He frowned. "The only problem is we couldn't find Drysi anywhere. I tried a tracking spell, but it didn't work." His expression turned grim.

If he's trying to track her instead of her body, the spell would have failed, but she might be alive and have blocked any tracking. Not only does she have access to her own spells, if she had a hidden flying artifact, she might have something that blocks tracking, too.

Whatever the truth was, she didn't want to talk about the witch's true nature yet. A few minutes of stability wasn't selfish.

"Drysi...helped me on the mountain." Alison frowned.

"Helped you?" he asked, his eyes filled with suspicion. "There's something you're not telling me."

Why do you have to be so good at reading me?

A few passing Nereids nodded politely to her.

"I'll explain later, once I've processed everything," she replied. "It's complicated. I thought I knew what was going on with her, but I had no fucking clue at all. Still, the important thing is that she helped me with the trident."

Hana turned her head a few times, obviously in search of the witch. She looked quizzically at Alison. "Wait. Two questions. First, how did she get up there? Second, where is she now?"

"Question one is easy—a magical flying umbrella."

The other woman's eyes and grin widened. "You are so shitting me. Seriously? A magical flying umbrella? So she's like a Welsh Mary Poppins?"

"Yeah, something like that. She even said that." She allowed herself a chuckle. "As for the second question..."

Hana gasped. "She didn't make it?"

She shook her head. "I don't think so, but I'm not sure."

"Damn," Mason muttered. "What a damned waste."

Alison nodded. "It was, and not even for the reasons you think." She sighed. "I suppose it's time I told you what happened up there. We'd better find Der. This involves the Nereids as well."

Alison strolled barefoot along the beach, enjoying the sand beneath her toes. Mason walked beside her but they'd not said much in the last half-hour other than Mason's initial question if she wanted to go for a walk. A day had passed since she had stopped the trident.

"We should consider going on a vacation," she suggested finally to break the silence. "Maybe after all the dark wizard crap is taken care of. Now that we have a lead, I figure it'll move quicker."

He nodded. "Setting that aside, do you seriously want to go on a vacation?"

"Yeah, just the two of us. Sonya can stay with Hana and Tahir for a week or two without it being too bad." Alison smiled. "And I mean a real vacation, not a his and hers ass-kicking adventure."

"His and hers ass-kicking?" Mason arched an eyebrow.

"Something my parents used to do. Occasionally, they still do." She shrugged. "It's like they're afraid that if they don't shoot something together, it'll hurt their marriage."

"We can go on a regular vacation," he replied. "It doesn't have to be a his and hers ass-kicking."

She grinned. "Do you regret getting involved with a woman who has such a weird family?"

"They helped make you into the woman I love, so no, I don't regret it at all." He looked over his shoulder at a Nereid who gathered driftwood in the distance. "It's as good as time as any to talk about this. When I talked to Der right before the walk, she said from the best they could tell using their spells, Drysi's body isn't on the island. They found Ine's, though. They have some ritual to return her to the sea they will do, but they made it clear it's a private matter."

"Fair enough." Alison sighed. "So Drysi might be alive—or she might have been obliterated for all we know." She stopped and examined several uprooted cypress trees up ahead. It would take a long time for the island to fully recover from the ravages of the storm.

She stared off at the ocean. Even though she'd success-fully bound the trident, Der hadn't reactivated the normal storm. Instead, she'd deactivated it entirely. Nereid Island was no longer a paradise hidden by a deadly and unnavigable storm.

"I don't know how to feel about her, Mason," she admitted.

"Drysi?"

"Yeah. She literally waited around and plotted to kill me, but she wasn't the one who released a seedpod or blew the plane up. She's the one who helped stop the trident." She shrugged. "Complicated legacies and all that crap."

Mason looked thoughtful. "Ine might be dead, but she accomplished her goal in a way."

"What do you mean?"

He gestured to the horizon. "They've shut the storm down. Aeternum will have a much larger presence on the island, along with the EU and UN. With all that extra help, the Nereids won't have to spend so much time worrying about the Curse Flowers. Even if they can't go elsewhere right away and survive, they might at least be able to have someone to portal them to kemanas or something."

"Most of the Nereids are satisfied here. Do you think that will change?"

"I think it's one thing when you believe you *have* to stay somewhere and another when you think you have options. More contact with the outside world is bound to make a lot of them more curious. I think it's inevitable that some will leave the island."

Alison gestured to the Nereid still busy with her clean up. "Maybe they have the right idea. Simple lives and simple pleasures."

"It's hard to say. Ine couldn't handle it." Mason shrugged. "I don't think I could, either. Maybe my big city perspective is too entrenched to change now. I don't know whether that's good or bad, but it's how I feel."

"Other than when I went to school, I've always lived in big cities," she mused. "I don't know if I could make the lifestyle adjustment either, but it's hard not to think about the possibilities and also, how they affect other people. My dad probably would have been happier for most of his life living alone in the woods with his dog, but because he didn't, he met Mom and me and now, I think he's happier than he ever was."

"Even the Seers couldn't exactly describe the future, so us non-Seers shouldn't worry too much."

She shook her head. "How long do you plan to live?"

Mason laughed. "Long enough? Longer than tomorrow but shorter than forever."

"Why not forever?"

"Because it'd be boring. What? Do you plan to live forever?" He smirked.

Alison locked eyes with him. "I'm serious. You're a life wizard. It's not like you'll die young."

"Why are you suddenly asking about this?" His expression alternated between concerned and amused.

"You mentioned perspective, and that reminded me of something." She kicked at the sand. "It's something Myna mentioned to me when I told her yet again that I wasn't interested in becoming the Queen of the Drow and that I'd be terrible at it. I told her that I basically had a human and an Earth perspective. She gave me a big speech about how long I would live and how my perspective would change with time, and she'd trust me to do the right thing or whatever when I was older."

"Sure." Mason shrugged. "It's no big deal though. Everyone's bound to change their opinions on some things as they get older."

A crab scuttled past, oblivious to the philosophical musings of a wizard bodyguard and his Drow princess girlfriend.

"Everyone?" she asked.

"Yeah, many non-magicals change their opinions as they get older, so there's no reason why magicals won't. Even teenagers have different opinions than they did as little kids. That doesn't mean you'll change your opinion about the Drow stuff, but who knows?" He shrugged.

She pointed to the mountains. "I keep going back to what Ine said. She was blessed with centuries of life, and she found it to be nothing but a curse—one so awful that she was willing to kill dozens of her own people to escape it."

Mason frowned. "Because she wasn't satisfied with life here. No one will make you live in any one place."

"I suppose, but Myna's little walkabout was because she was dissatisfied after centuries of living, too."

"Because she was an exile and Queen Laena was a bitch. Think about all those library gnomes. After thousands of years doing the same job, they're satisfied. It's not about the age but about how you think about it."

"It does make sense when you put it that way." She took his arm and leaned her head against his shoulder. "The only thing I know is that I'll continue to fight to protect people. You have to understand that will never change, even if I live to two thousand."

"Why would I ask you to change?" Mason looked

confused. "And if I'm still around with you after two thousand years, I'm obviously doing something right."

Alison chuckled. "The point is that sometimes, to protect people, I have to risk my own life, and that won't change. I won't ever hide from the Mountain Strider who threatens the neighborhood or the dark wizard assassins who threaten my friends." She held a hand up to stop his response. "Yes, I know that I'm not the only strong magical in the world, but that's all the more reason for me to do my part. Every one of us is a light and we can push back against the darkness. Maybe we can't get rid of it, but we can at least shove it into a closet somewhere."

He laughed. "I liked that metaphor right up until the end."

"Really? I thought it was impressive."

"Don't quit the day job, but from everything you said, it sounds like you need a good bodyguard. I could make a recommendation or two."

She winked. "I know a guy. He's handsome and a good painter, too. But he'll have to be able to put up with a self-righteous woman who overthinks things."

"He sounds great. You should hire him and move in with him immediately. I'm sure he'll be able to handle you well."

"Maybe." She smiled. "We'll see how things go."

Two days later, Alison couldn't sleep as they headed toward Lisbon on a new plane. It took considerable combined magical effort to get the runway ready, but it was easier than waiting for a boat.

The first thing I should do when we get home is figure out how to cast a spell where I'll slap myself if I ever say aloud that a job will be easy.

Everyone else on the plane was asleep with the exception of Abigail, who sat across the small aisle in the charter plane and read messages on her phone, her brow furrowed. Nearly getting killed didn't mean she didn't have a world to return to.

The woman had impressed Alison with her calm. Even the previous assassination attempt on her life was nothing like what she'd gone through on Nereid Island. The way she'd kept her composure throughout the entire incident had given the security team one less major thing to worry about.

She looked at the CEO. "How are you doing? Is everything okay?"

Abigail raised her head. "I'm still alive, which means I'm doing better than many people, including Kenneth." She sighed and shook her head.

The plane shook slightly with turbulence.

"I'm sorry about Kenneth," she said quietly. "I don't think I've had a chance to say that since we stopped Ine and the storm. I'm also sorry for thinking he blew the plane up and released the seedpod. It's a weak defense, but I'm a security contractor, not a detective."

The other woman sighed. "But do you think it's true?"

She shook her head. "No, not at all. Ine was clearly responsible. He didn't have anything to do with those incidents."

"That's not what I'm talking about. You found all that other evidence on his phone. Do you think he was sympathetic with the New Veil?"

Alison shrugged. "I don't know. We only know what we found on that phone, and it wasn't all that specific. He might have been a sympathizer, or perhaps he simply researched them because he found the idea interesting intellectually."

"To be honest, he didn't seem like the kind of man who had an intellectual interest in such things, which makes me inclined to believe he was sympathetic—even if he never showed it before or mentioned it to me."

"It might have been the Carlyle trial, or it might have been the passage of time. I've met people who have grown to hate magic, and I've met magic haters who now love the idea of it. It's hard to say."

Abigail frowned and stared down at her phone. "You think you know people, but you really don't. It makes me wonder how many employees I have who harbor some sort of deep hatred that I don't know about."

"My dad was a bounty hunter, and I was a bounty hunter before I did security contracting. I think it's helped me to understand a lot about the world and the people in it."

The woman scoffed. "Did it teach you that the world's full of scum who prey on the innocent?"

"That's true, but I knew that from before I was a bounty hunter. My biological mother was tortured to death by gangsters, after all."

Abigail's expression softened. "I'm sorry."

"It's all right," she responded. She glanced over as

Mason stirred in his sleep and continued once he settled. "But the more I think about it, the more I think the most important lesson I learned was at my magic school."

"And what was that?" the CEO asked, her face full of genuine curiosity.

"Everyone has the potential for lightness and darkness." Alison shrugged. "Ine wasn't evil because she hated everyone. She was desperate and misguided. Because she thought she was trapped, she lashed out. Drysi had helped horrible people and done awful things, but she still gave her money away out of a sense of duty, and when the time came to make the right choice, she did."

Abigail chuckled. "You're very wise for someone so young, but then again, I suppose you've dealt with more in your short life than most humans will ever deal with in their entire lives."

"That's true, even if it's something of a curse."

"If I don't hear about curses for ten years, it'll be too soon." The woman grimaced.

"I can't say that I disagree. I hope the EU and UN can help the Nereids do something about the Curse Flowers. I'm sure the Oricerans have some ideas. They must have had to clean stuff like that up before."

"I'm inclined to agree, but I'll leave that to the experts." Abigail leaned back in her seat and closed her eyes. "I'm glad I hired Brownstone Security for this job. Otherwise, who knows what might have happened? If you'll excuse me, I'd like to get a little sleep before we land, and now that you've broken me out of the spell of my work phone, I'm tired."

"Go ahead."

Drysi was a dark wizard, but she wasn't responsible for what happened on the island and more importantly, she gave me a name.

Her breath caught.

She gave me a damned name.

CHAPTER TWENTY-SIX

Alison knocked on the door to the office Tahir shared with Sonya. The girl wasn't there that day as she was participating in an official drone battle race. It didn't matter, as she wasn't there to talk to the young infomancer.

Tahir looked up from his computer. "I didn't say you needed to come immediately in my message. Weren't you still eating lunch?" He looked more surprised than apologetic.

"I was, but you said the magic words in the text." She closed the door behind her. "You said you had information on Conrad Barnes. My sandwich can wait a few minutes if you have what I need to take down one of the bastards who sent people to kill my friends and has made Izzie's life hell."

He chuckled quietly. "Indeed, I do have information, but let me first set appropriate limits on your excitement. I found considerable information on the man, but it's not the information that you want. It's not as actionable as you would desire."

"What does that mean?" She frowned. "Is the guy officially dead or something?"

"No, not at all. In fact, he's a respected wizard and businessman in UK circles. I did confirm that he lives in London, but he's hidden any of his more objectionable dealings extremely and unusually well." The infomancer sniffed disdainfully. "Much of his personal affairs are rather analog or magical but not electronic, which complicates things for both me and him. Obviously, he won't bring his cellphone to one of the Seventh Order meetings and stream it to social media."

Alison scowled. Nothing Tahir said was surprising, but that didn't stop it from being annoying.

"So he likes to hide stuff?" she replied. "If he takes those kinds of measures, it sounds like he's the kind of man who doesn't want his terrorist actions to be discovered. But it doesn't matter."

"It doesn't matter? How does his effective concealment of incriminating evidence not matter?"

"Because it's not like we've not run into rich bastards who aren't good at hiding shit." She scoffed. "And now, both billionaires who messed with us are in prison. I don't need enough to convict Barnes. I simply need to go at him."

Tahir tapped a few commands and read a pop-up alert on his screen. "The man's schedule is rather secretive. That's another thing that is very suspicious and also complicates potential efforts. He uses what appear to be body doubles, either real or illusionary, far more than one would suspect for a simple businessman." He tapped on his keyboard and brought up an article. "A possible explanation or a set-up excuse for a dangerous man to employ extreme defenses without being questioned."

ASSASSINATION ATTEMPT ON BRITISH BUSI-NESSMAN FOILED.

Alison nodded at the screen. "What's this about?"

"Allegedly, a witch assassin attempted to murder him years ago," he explained. "He's used it as an excuse for his unusual level of security."

"He'll need a *lot* of security to stop me."

Tahir stared at her, slight condescension in his gaze. "Here's the problem as I see it. You simply can't go after this man, especially in England where you have fewer connections with law enforcement. The only evidence you have against him is the testimony of a confessed dark witch murderer. If you attack him, you'll probably end up with a bounty on you."

"I also won't sit around and do nothing."

"I'm not saying you should. I'm simply noting that you'll need more evidence before you go after him so you don't end up on the run like Izzie. If he's one of the leaders of the group behind all these incidents, he won't be someone whose door you can simply kick down or eliminate with ease. He's also not Carlyle."

Alison's gaze flicked from Tahir to the computer screen. "I know he's not Carlyle."

"What I'm getting at is that as an experienced wizard, he'll have many different ways to deal with you that aren't sheer brute force technology and technomagic, or even suave manipulation. He is, by his very nature, a much more dangerous threat than Carlyle."

"Duly noted." She took a few deep breaths to quell her

galloping heart. She'd convinced herself on the way to
Tahir's office that she'd be able to go after Conrad within
days. Her hands curled into fists with the frustration.

*It doesn't matter. I'm still in a better position than I was
before Drysi gave me the information. I need to keep telling
myself that.*

The infomancer clicked his mouse a few times. "Now
that we have the name, we can keep an eye on him and his
activities to gather more evidence and decide on the best
way to strike. But I also think there's something else you
should keep in mind before you plan anything that
involves you crashing through his front window with your
shadow blade."

"And what might that be?"

Tahir brought up a news article about the fight at the
Lincoln Memorial. "Given the tactics we've seen from
these dark wizards, including the use of group cells and
compartmentalization, you won't want to strike at any
leader until you're sure you won't lose leads on the others.
The organization—the Seventh Order—seems to be what
you need to focus on here, not only the individuals. Prema-
ture moves could backfire."

Alison thought about the earlier story about the assassination attempt. She half-wondered if the so-called witch
assassin was Izzie.

*She needs to know this, but it'll be at least a few weeks before
she contacts me again.*

"Then we shouldn't pass it along to the PDA either,"
Alison observed. "Even if the local office is clean, they
might pass the report up the chain and then we'll never
catch this guy with his pants down, given how paranoid he

is already. You're right, Tahir. This isn't only about kicking some ass. We need to burn this Seventh Order to the ground and make such a display that the dark wizard families don't even dare to look in my or Izzie's direction again. We'll make them the ones afraid and on the run, and that will take planning."

He nodded. "I agree. I know that isn't immediately satisfying, but it's the best strategy in the long run. Their tactics haven't always been effective, but we could learn a thing or two from their long-term subtle planning."

"Satisfying? Oh, that doesn't matter. Knowing now that we'll be able to go directly after one of them in the future is satisfaction enough." Her smile turned hungry. "Gathering intelligence is going on the offensive, and I'm glad we're finally not stuck on defense."

She flipped her scallops and smiled at the perfect sear. Her grin widened as she inhaled, loving the aroma. "It's almost ready."

Not bad. It's been a long time since I fucked up a scallop.

Mason smiled from the table. "Take your time, A. I'm enjoying the smell enough as it is."

"Hey, if you could go anywhere on vacation, where would you go?" She plated the scallops.

"I honestly don't know." He scratched his chin. "I've seen a lot of the world as a bodyguard, but I've never been to Oriceran. Maybe there."

"I visited the Drow, which was interesting, but I feel like I should see more of my own planet before I spend a lot of time visiting the other. It'll make both experiences stronger in contrast." She checked the clock. It'd be a few more minutes before the Beef Wellington was ready.

He laughed. "I do know one place I don't want to go anytime soon."

"Where's that?"

"Any remote islands, even if they are tropical."

"Very funny." Alison picked the plates up and marched into the dining room. She set Mason's in front of him and hers down at her place. "About ten more minutes in the oven and then a few for resting for the Wellington." She picked a fork up. "That's why I pounded the scallops out as an appetizer."

"They look great." He took a bite, chewed thoughtfully, and swallowed. "They taste great, too."

"Thanks." She all but inhaled hers, far hungrier than she'd realized.

"There's another option," he pointed out after another mouthful.

"Another option?"

Mason nodded. "Yes. A staycation. I'm sure we could find things to entertain us." He waggled his eyebrows.

She snickered. "Down, boy. We can do that anywhere." She blew out a breath. "I don't know. Maybe I'll call Mom and ask for suggestions. Dad always says the same thing when I ask him, 'Well, there's this barbecue place...'" She rolled her eyes and laughed.

"It's good to see you happy, A. I know you have a lot on your mind, and I know that what went down with Drysi gnaws at you."

Alison shook her head. "Whether she's still alive in hiding or dead, it actually doesn't."

He looked surprised. "It doesn't?"

"She did the right thing in the end, and that's all that matters to me. I didn't know the witch who helped dark wizards. I knew the bounty hunter who was outraged about trafficking." She drew a deep breath. "She was misguided, but I do think she genuinely cared about injustice, and if even a dark wizard assassin can have that in common with me, then the future's not hopeless."

"That's a good way to look at it."

"For now, I'll keep doing what I'm doing." Alison snapped her fingers. "I forgot the wine." She stood. "I'll get it."

Seattle or some island, I'm still me. I have a great boyfriend, a great team at work, and all the tools I need to kick ass.

Drysi, if you're still out there, I promise you that I'll do what I can to push back at the asses trying to choke this world with their greed and corruption.

Conrad, somehow, I bet you're not worried about giving money to struggling families. Enjoy your last little time as the hunter rather than the hunted. When you attacked my building, you broke the most important rule.

"Don't ever go after someone a Brownstone cares about."

The story is far from over. Alison's adventure continues in
THE QUEEN'S DAUGHTER.

FREE BOOKS!

Join the only newsletter hosted by a Troll!

Get sneak peeks, exclusive giveaways, behind the scenes
content, and more.
PLUS you'll be notified of special **one day only fan
pricing** on new releases.

CLICK HERE

or visit: https://marthacarr.com/read-free-stories/

The story is far from over. Alison's adventure continues in THE QUEEN'S DAUGHTER.

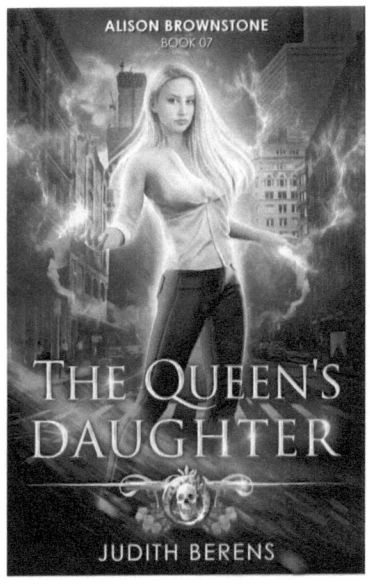

AVAILABLE AT AMAZON RETAILERS

I'm not a big fan of change – I'm in a very large club, I know. And yet, life is a constant series of changes, especially if you're chasing a dream or another adventure. Check and check on both items. That means I'm constantly agreeing to let go of what I do know, what I've grown comfortable with, to reach for something new.

Like starting Oriceran Universe with Michael Anderle or moving into my dream house or quitting my day job and who knows what's coming next.

New territory that I've never seen before so I have no point of reference and can't know exactly how things will go. This is where there's an urge to turn back to what's familiar out of a false sense of safety. Fortunately, I've learned a few coping skills.

The first one is I don't let the conversation with just myself go on too long before I call someone. But not just anyone... I'm careful to only call people who know that eventually things work out and operate off that belief. That means they're going to let me talk it out – once- and then we're on to reality. What is actually happening – not what have I imagined might happen (also known as magical thinking). In that present moment all is well and what I really need to do is recognize that nothing is wrong, and I've made a solid plan and well frankly, I can't control the rest. But I can trust and just go forward. If things need adjusting later, that will be apparent and I know who to go to for advice or assistance.

Last step is some gratitude. It's hard to worry and be grateful at the same time, and there's a lot to be grateful for if I'm willing to start looking in that direction instead. All the rest I let go of and get on with whatever the next thing there is to do, even if it's playing with the dogs or creating magic on the page. It's a good life and I'm glad I get to do it with so many great Fans, sharing the journey.

This weekend I'll be opening up the new house to 9 other authors – our first summit – to go over what we can each contribute, what problem we would love to solve, and what we hope to accomplish in 2019. I'm creating a small, intimate hive mind that can keep on helping each other throughout the year. More change – I'm ready for it. See you on the flip side. More adventures to follow.

THANK YOU for not only reading this story but these *Author Notes* as well.

RANDOM (*sometimes*) THOUGHTS?

If you had a choice of what type of fantasy / paranormal creature you could be, how long would you take to think about it?

When I was younger, I would have immediately said magic user. It's the most obvious choice, right? Throwing around fireballs and casting sleep spells on your enemies seems like great choice.

Unfortunately, now that I'm older I recognize the incredible need to pay attention to the details about how the magic user gains their spells.

Is it simple sleep? Do they have to meditate on the spells each morning? Do they have to have the right spell components?

Because, if they do I'd be screwed. I'm neither good with meditation nor the boy scout effort of being prepared.

Nope.

So, now that I know my personality isn't suited to magic user I would have to spend more time thinking about my options. I think I could deal with being a cleric unless there are food limitations regarding steak, pizza, bbq, and Coke.

Ok, let's try fighter.

No, absolutely not. Too much exercise needed for that class.

I won't bore you with the details, but I'm starting to come to the conclusion that I would choose fantasy author with a +10 to typing speed.

And be happy.

AROUND THE WORLD IN 80 DAYS

Las Vegas, Nevada (Condo writing in bed.)

I was going to come to bed way early, get my iPad and read or just sleep. I'm still suffering from coming back from London a few days ago and I'm sleeeeeeepy.

Then I remembered I had author notes to accomplish before tomorrow morning.

I'm typing as my eyes try to close and so far I'm winning the battle to stay awake.

I'm stopping now to get this to Steve so I can go to sleep.

THANK YOU for reading these notes and I'm sorry for sucking so bad with these notes this evening.

FAN PRICING

$0.99 Saturdays (new LMBPN stuff) and $0.99 Wednesday (both LMBPN books and friends of LMBPN books.) Get great stuff from us and others at tantalizing prices.

Go ahead, I bet you can't read just one.

Sign up here: http://lmbpn.com/email/.

HOW TO MARKET FOR BOOKS YOU LOVE

Review them so others have your thoughts, tell friends and the dogs of your enemies (because who wants to talk with enemies?)... *Enough said ;-)*

Ad Aeternitatem,

Michael Anderle

OTHER SERIES IN THE ORICERAN
UNIVERSE:

SCHOOL OF NECESSARY MAGIC
SCHOOL OF NECESSARY MAGIC: RAINE CAMPBELL
ALISON BROWNSTONE
THE DANIEL CODEX SERIES
THE LEIRA CHRONICLES
I FEAR NO EVIL
THE UNBELIEVABLE MR. BROWNSTONE
REWRITING JUSTICE
THE KACY CHRONICLES
MIDWEST MAGIC CHRONICLES
SOUL STONE MAGE
THE FAIRHAVEN CHRONICLES

OTHER BOOKS BY JUDITH BERENS

OTHER BOOKS BY MARTHA CARR

JOIN THE ORICERAN UNIVERSE FAN GROUP ON
FACEBOOK!

CONNECT WITH THE AUTHORS

Martha Carr Social

Website: http://www.marthacarr.com

Facebook: https://www.facebook.com/
groups/MarthaCarrFans/

Michael Anderle Social

Michael Anderle Social
Website:
http://www.lmbpn.com

Email List:
http://lmbpn.com/email/

Facebook Here: https://www.
facebook.com/TheKurtherianGambitBooks/